Last winter was warm. I remember the cherry trees had already started to blossom by this time last year. Grandma was no longer able to urinate and fluid began to pool in her stomach. After the doctor warned us that she did not have long to live, she was in a coma for weeks, and the fluid in her stomach gradually pushed its way up, until, darkened by blood, it oozed from her mouth. My mother stayed at the hospital day after day, pushing gauze pads into her mouth to soak up the fluid that seeped out with a gurgling sound. For many days the wastebasket had been filled with pads stained deep red. Then I had the thought, "Grandma would be better off dead."

Although I did not want to think such a thing, although I had told her so many times that I wanted her to live forever, I went ahead and thought, "Grandma would be better off dead."

And the next day, at noon, she died. She died because of my thought. I never wanted her to die. I wanted her to be there always. Forever and ever, by my side. I know that my wish was sincere. But still she died.

That was when I began having nightmares about turning into a monster.

The Spring Tone

KAZUMI YUMOTO

Translated by CATHY HIRANO

The Spring Tone

The original Japanese edition edited by Rei Uemura

Published by
Dell Laurel-Leaf
an imprint of
Random House Children's Books
a division of Random House, Inc.
1540 Broadway
New York, New York 10036

Visit us on the Web! www.randomhouse.com/teens

Educators and librarians, for a variety of teaching tools, visit us at www.randomhouse.com/teachers

ISBN: 0-440-22855-7

RL: 5.3

Reprinted by arrangement with Farrar, Straus and Giroux

Printed in the United States of America

April 2001

10 9 8 7 6 5 4 3 2 1

OPM

The Spring Tone

One

"Look out! A monster! A monster is coming!"

People run away from me, screaming. I have no idea what I look like—from what they are saying I can only assume that I am indeed a monster. But from their tone of voice I can tell that they are jeering at me, and I am annoyed.

"Run! Run! Look how slow it is! It can't catch you if you run!" Some boy, a stranger, comes right up to me and sticks out his tongue. Then he runs away. I couldn't catch him, even if I tried. My body feels too heavy, like a fish floundering on dry land. I can't even make my arms move. So instead I roar, a great and terrible roar, from the very pit of my stomach. I stand still, shut my eyes, and scream with all my might, as if spewing out all the poison that is churning within me. It feels good. This time, everyone trembles with terror. Filled with satisfaction, I scream on and on.

Then they are gone, and the voices crying "Monster!" fade away. I am all alone, yet I continue to scream. After all, I never chose to be a monster.

"What's the scariest thing in the world?" a voice asks, and I float upward as if my body has suddenly become completely empty. But only for a moment. I open my eyes.

I don't want to wake up. What good would it do me? Like a crocodile sinking slowly under the mud, I slither back into a dream. *Glub, glub, glub* . . .

"Sharks." The voice comes from the bottom bunk of our bunk bed.

Sharks? Where? No. It's only my younger brother, Tetsu.

"Sharks are definitely the scariest."

I recall my dream. I've been having this sort of dream a lot lately.

"How about you?" Tetsu asks me.

The scariest thing in the world . . . "Monsters," I reply.

"What kind?"

"I don't know."

"Hmm." Tetsu grunts and then mutters to himself that nothing could be more terrifying than to be eaten by a shark.

"Stay away from the ocean, then."

"Mm, yeah. But what if I was flying in an airplane and it crashed into the sea?"

I think of retorting that he should stay away from airplanes, too, but decide against it. Instead I pull the covers over my head.

The graduation ceremony yesterday was a disaster. I was class representative, which meant that I had to go up onto the stage and receive everyone's diplomas on behalf of my class, but at the beginning of the ceremony I began to feel ill. "It must have been that piece of pineapple I ate for breakfast," I thought as I listened to each name being read.

"And Tomomi Kiriki, representative of the aforementioned thirty-nine members of the graduating class." I heard my name called and began to walk toward the front. My forehead ached. I trod carefully up the stairs to the stage and stood in front of the principal while he read my graduation certificate out loud. My head felt as if it was being slowly squeezed in a vise. Taking the diplomas, I bowed, then turned to face the auditorium. The heads of the people in the audience seemed to heave like a black wave. Where were my mother and father? Although my eyes were wide open, I couldn't see a thing. The black wave crashed over me and swallowed me up.

Afterward, I was told that I had fainted, falling backward as stiff as a board, like someone in a cartoon—*crash!*—scattering the diplomas all over.

To make matters worse, Mr. Noguchi, the physical education instructor, carried me to the nurse's room. He is a real creep. He makes us skip rope in gym class so he can stare at the chests of the girls who are starting to develop. The doctor advised me to skip rope at home every day because the headaches I've been having lately are caused by poor circulation. But that would remind me of Mr. Noguchi's face, and I would rather die.

"If I had a pet shark, I'd tell him to eat that creep." This time Tetsu's voice snaps me awake. Creep? What creep? Who is he talking about? Mr. Noguchi? Can he read my mind? I lean over the side of the bed and look down at Tetsu lying under the covers, reading a dog-eared encyclopedia.

"What creep?" I ask, but at that moment the door bursts open.

"If you're awake, then hurry up and get out of bed."

My mother. Not only does she never knock, she doesn't even say good morning. Lying on my side, I wave goodbye.

"How's your head?" she asks, looking intently at my face. "You look a bit pale."

"It feels like my headache's coming back," I say, snuggling under the covers. "You do know that spring break starts today, don't you?" Spring break lasts a little less than two weeks, and then the new school year starts the first week in April. And we won't have another break—for summer vacation—until the middle of July. And once school starts again at the beginning of September, we won't have a vacation until December 24. Just thinking about it makes me exhausted. I want to sleep as much as I can.

My mother sighs and mutters something about my needing to stop being so lazy. Then she says, "At least take the garbage out, would you? I can't carry all of it myself." And, as usual, she rushes out the door like a whirlwind, heading for the office.

I feel as if I am just hanging in midair. Perhaps I am too lazy.

During summer vacation last year, I did not go swimming even once. In the fall, I stopped playing with my friends. I quit piano lessons around Christmas. I think I started getting headaches a little before that. Then I was demoted from the top class in my cram school, where I had been studying every day after school in preparation for the junior-high entrance exams. I should have set my sights a little lower right then and there, and chosen another school to try to get into, but I kept thinking that if I just worked a little harder I could get back on track. But despite rushing to cram school every evening with my brain growing fuzzier and fuzzier, all I have to show for my efforts is my failure to pass the exams for the two schools I wanted to go to.

Like the pendulum of a clock that is winding down, I am gradually grinding to a complete halt.

I carry the garbage outside. The sky is overcast; everything is gray. Gray clouds that look as if they might produce snow at any minute, cold gray light, gray telephone poles, gray concrete, gray . . . What is that? Something gray is lying at the side of the road.

Its legs stick out stiff and straight, its eyes and mouth are tightly shut. It must have been hit by a car, but there is no blood. A big gray cat. Its legs, even its tail, are very stubby.

I poke it gingerly with the tip of one finger, but the body beneath the soft fur is like stone. It feels cold.

"What's that?" Tetsu asks as he brings out the other garbage bags. His straggly bangs stick up like the tassels on a corn

7

husk, his shirt is buttoned wrong and is hanging out of his pants, and despite the cold he is wearing neither a sweater nor socks. He looks like someone who has just been rescued from the middle of a raging windstorm.

"Is it dead?"

I remark that it must have been hit by a car, and he says, "When cats are startled by a car's headlights, they freeze in their tracks. That's why they get hit."

"You sure know a lot about it."

"I read it in a book."

I should have known. "All you ever talk about are things that you've read in an encyclopedia or a dictionary or something."

"It's a male."

"How do you know?"

"Look. He's got those." Tetsu points. At the base of the cat's tail are two plump round balls, like fur-covered cherries. "I bet he was a tough old tomcat. He probably came here to expand his territory."

"Do cats have territories?"

Tetsu nods solemnly. "What should we do with it?" he asks, his eyes still glued to the corpse.

"I'll tell Grandpa so he can report it."

"Where?"

"I don't know. The Sanitation Department or someplace like that, I guess."

Once, when I was little, I saw a dog that had been hit by a car. Two men wearing coveralls came in a truck to take it away, and although I did not ask, they told me, "Look at that. It's wearing a collar. Stupid dog. It must have panicked and dashed out into the street because it got lost." It was a short-haired white dog, so thin that it looked naked. Staring at its rigid corpse, I began to feel as if I had been hit by the car myself, and that the two men were lifting my body. My head began to spin. I seemed to have become one with the dog and they were about to take me away . . . For the next few days, I kept pinching and hitting myself just to make sure I was still alive. That was the first time I ever saw a living creature that had died.

"Can I have it?" Tetsu asks, looking up at me from where he is crouching beside the cat.

"What!"

"Well, why not, if you're just going to call someone to take it away?" Tetsu drags a sheet of cardboard from the garbage pile and pushes at the cat's fat back with his fingertips, nudging it along until he somehow manages to maneuver it onto the cardboard. Carrying it carefully like a tray, he stands up, his elbows trembling under the weight. A tiny thread of blood drips like drool from the cat's mouth.

"What are you going to do?"

Tetsu staggers back into our yard without answering.

"Tetsu!" What can he be thinking? I grab the garbage bags, including Tetsu's.

After breakfast, as soon as I have washed the dishes, I head straight upstairs. Tetsu is on his bed, looking at an encyclopedia again. This time he's reading about airplanes. He is probably researching which airplanes are least likely to fall into shark-infested oceans.

"So what are you planning to do with that cat?"

Tetsu starts humming.

"All right, then. I guess you won't mind if I tell Grandpa."

"Tomomi."

"Yeah?"

"You tried one of Grandpa's cigarettes the other day, didn't you?"

"I just lit it, that's all."

"What did it taste like?"

"Awful."

"Hmm."

"I put it out right away."

"But if Mom finds out, you'll be in big trouble, right?"

I decide to keep quiet. After all, Tetsu wouldn't keep a cat corpse in a dresser drawer, or anything. At least, I don't think he would . . . I catch myself chewing my nails again. This is boring. What can we do to have fun? Nothing comes to mind.

"Tetsu. You want to play Othello?"

"Nah."

"I'll let you go first."

"Not right now." He won't even look up from his book.

I go downstairs and check the laundry room, but all the clothes have been put away. I open the fridge absently and wander aimlessly about the house until I find myself standing in the doorway of the storage room.

Not that there is anything particularly interesting in there.

Grandma's bureau, darkened with age; a three-sided mirror that still bears the marks of stickers I pasted on it when I was little; a chest full of Grandpa's shiny old suits; a dusty glass case filled with ornaments; an old coffee jar stuffed with buttons; an outdated set of encyclopedias. The room is packed so full of musty-smelling things that there is barely room to stand.

But today I notice something different: my mother's old organ. It is in the farthest corner, draped with a moth-eaten blanket and wedged between a bookcase and a chest of drawers. If the straw hat that I bought at the beach the summer before last had not been sitting on top, I might never have noticed it. I seem to remember that I loved to play with the organ when I was little because you could select three different types of sound.

I take off the blanket and gently lift the cool, black lid. When I plug the organ in and turn on the switch, it starts to hum even though I am not touching the keys. I place my ear close to it, and realize that each key is faintly ringing. The sound reminds me of the noise from a distant expressway on a winter morning, the vibration gradually becoming more distinct, like a myriad multicolored rings spinning outward, around and around.

The room has been closed all winter. In the cold damp with that persistent noise ringing in my ears, I'm sure I am going to get another headache.

"Oh, that organ's no good anymore."

My grandfather comes in, forcing his stout figure between the chest of drawers and the bookcase. He has an unlit cigarette clamped between his teeth. "It's no good," he repeats to himself and stretches out his hand, reaching for the switch.

A great clap of thunder peals, or so it seems to me. The noise, however, comes from the organ, as though it is trying to strike my grandfather's hand away, crying, *"Don't touch that switch!"*

Grandpa snatches his hand back in surprise, then reaches in front of me for the switch, so we are both stuck in the cramped space. The noise stops for a moment, but then resurges, growing louder and louder until I think it will never end. When it finally does, I can feel all the tension drain from Grandpa's body.

"This was Mom's when she was a kid, wasn't it?" I ask.

Grandpa nods. "No wonder it doesn't work. That was a long time ago." He kneels down and pulls out the plug. The quiet drone of the organ is stilled and the sudden hush makes me feel as if my ears are stuffed with cotton wool. "Guess I'd better tidy things up in here," Grandpa says.

"You mean clean out the storage room?"

He doesn't answer. Lighting his cigarette and puffing out clouds of smoke, he takes a book from the bookcase and starts looking at it.

"If you stay in here, your knees will start hurting again," I warn him.

A chill rain has been falling for days now, and this room, which was added on next to the bathroom after the house was built, is especially damp. The old sliding paper doors bulge with moisture, and where they are torn you can see the layers

12

inside peeling like puff pastry. This burning sensation in my nose must be from all the dust.

"Mom said she's going to get rid of all this stuff anyway when we rebuild the house."

But Grandpa continues to smoke his cigarette and separate the old books, the covers of which are stuck together, one by one. He stops occasionally to cough violently, and smoke belches out of his mouth, as from a machine that's about to break down. Stubborn old man! He just goes right ahead and does whatever he wants. He never explains or makes excuses, and he never listens to anyone else's opinion. That is why he won't cut down on his smoking or go to a doctor about his cough. And that is why he is going to sit here in this moldy old room, spending his time with worthless junk. At times like this, I hate Grandpa.

"Grandpa's acting kind of strange lately, don't you think?" I remark to Tetsu.

His humming stops. There is no reply.

"He keeps wasting his time on useless jobs. Now he says he's going to clean out the storage room. It's ridiculous!"

Tetsu ignores me.

"At least he used to fix the leaks when it rained.

"He even made me a bookcase.

"He hasn't touched the garden for ages."

No answer. Tetsu is lying on his bed, with a book open as usual. There is no point in talking to him. He doesn't understand anything, anyway.

I take a compact mirror my mother gave me out of my desk drawer and gaze into it. I bring it close to my face and count my eyelashes, watching the pupils of my eyes dilate and contract. Usually when I do this, my irritation vanishes, as if my soul has been sucked into the mirror. Maybe it's because the compact mirror is so small it can't reflect any unnecessary details, unlike the big mirror in the bathroom.

But today is different. Too many things are bothering me.

I wonder what's wrong with Grandpa. And it's not just him, either. My father has retreated to the studio he rents for his translation work, and he only comes home occasionally to get a change of clothes.

"Everyone is acting strange," Tetsu comments out of the blue. I turn in surprise, but his face is hidden behind his book, so I can't see his expression.

"It's all that creep's fault," he says.

"What creep?" I ask, remembering Tetsu's earlier remark about feeding some creep to a shark.

"Who are you talking about?" I ask again.

There is no reply. But I don't want to think about it anyway, so I gaze into the mirror once more.

Two

I wonder where Tetsu hid that dead cat. He doesn't seem to be particularly uneasy, and he is certainly no less talkative than usual. And his topics of conversation are just as boring. Such as, "If a mongoose and a snake fought, which one do you think would win?" In other words, he's his normal self. The sun goes down the same as on any other day, and my mother comes home and we eat supper as always. Tetsu picks at his food as he does at every meal and only manages to eat about half of it after a lot of scolding from my mother, followed by more nagging to brush his teeth. We go to bed as usual, and I read a comic book for a while before turning out the bedside lamp and falling fast asleep until morning. Or so it should have been.

In the middle of the night, I wake up suddenly, though I have not been dreaming. Tetsu is moving about in the dark. Dazed with sleep, I strain my eyes and see him slipping out of the room. He is wearing a jacket over his pajamas, and, amazingly enough, he has socks on.

I think of calling out to him, but decide against it. Getting up quietly, I grab a jacket and go out into the hallway. Tiptoeing down the cold stairs, I hear the back door creak. He is going outside. But what for? Sleep has been completely banished from my brain.

The air outside is softer than I had anticipated. It may rain tomorrow, I think. But right now, although the moon isn't very big, it is so bright that I almost expect to hear it jingling like a silver sleigh bell. Tetsu is crouching down by the clothesline, pulling something out from between the garden wall and the shed. Holding my breath in the shadows, I hear the rustling sound of paper. Then Tetsu begins to climb the wall, carrying a bundle wrapped in newspaper.

The wall that divides our property from the neighbor's house on the north side has a rather complicated history. First there is the precast concrete wall that my grandfather had made when my mother was a child. Right smack up against it on the other side stands a tall cement-block wall built recently by the next-door neighbor. Thus it is a double wall. Tetsu climbs on top of our wall first. When he stands on this, the top of the neighbor's block wall is slightly lower than his navel. He gently places his bundle on top, then straddles the wall and maneuvers himself into a sitting position with his legs dangling over the other side. He clasps the bundle tightly to his chest, and his back, which has been heaving with exertion, seems to freeze. In the next instant, he vanishes.

The ground beneath our wall is dark with moss, neglected in the northernmost corner of the yard. It is only in the summer that the sun can reach below the second seam in the concrete at the bottom. I press my ear against the wall's cold dampness. I hear nothing.

The cherry tree in the neighbor's yard sways suddenly, and I step back. Tetsu's face reappears above the wall, looming over me, white in the moonlight. My heart skips a beat. His face is completely transformed and frightening. My aunt always says, "Tetsu is so fair. With that pale skin and those red lips, he looks just like Snow White. Too bad Tomomi didn't get his complexion instead." But now his face is completely drained of color—a white paper face with two holes cut out for eyes.

"What are you doing?" I demand when he reaches the ground. He is startled for a second, and then blinks his eyes, excited and pleased. I am a little relieved. Tetsu has not been transformed into a ghost, nor has he become a monster, as I do in my dream.

"The neighbor." Tetsu pulls a very crumpled newspaper from under his jacket. "I left the cat there."

"The cat? You mean the one from this morning?" My voice is shaking, and not just from the cold.

"Yup."

"You mean you left that dead cat in the neighbor's yard?"

"Yes." Walking past me, he runs his finger along the wooden slats of the shed wall as he heads toward the back door.

"What did you do that for?"

"Huh?" Tetsu turns toward me in the dark.

"What are you up to? I am certainly not going to have anything to do with it, whatever it is!"

Tetsu's face seems to float in the moonlight. His lips are firmly pressed together.

"Tomomi, you know what's been going on. It's all his fault."

I'd suspected as much, but now it is very clear who Tetsu has been referring to as "that creep." The old man next door. He lives with his wife, a meek, gentle-looking woman, and we often hear him yelling at her, even from our house. "And it's not just because she's hard-of-hearing," my mother has remarked. "He's always been like that." He spends most of the day puttering in the garden, so it is obvious who is going to find the dead cat tomorrow morning.

"He hates cats. I saw him once a long time ago."

"Saw him what?"

"A stray cat came into his yard and he sprayed it with pesticide. *Sssss.* Like that."

"Really?"

"Yes. He chased it all over." Tetsu falls silent for a moment. "It's a fitting revenge," he says seriously.

"But what are you going to do if he finds out?"

"No problem. He's just a big, fat liar, anyway."

I stare at him in astonishment. "A big, fat liar," he repeats.

The problem centers on that odd double wall. It all began a long time ago, when my mother was a child. There was no fence to mark the boundary between our property and our neighbor's house on the north side. When my mother took her first tottering steps, Grandpa decided to put up a wall so that she wouldn't stray into the neighbor's yard. But the contractor made a mistake and built the wall inside our property line, cutting about ten square yards off our land. Grandpa only realized this about a decade later. He and the neighbor talked it over and agreed that the wall could be moved when Grandpa decided to rebuild our house. And they left it at that, with Grandpa saying that it would be hard on our neighbor to suddenly find his garden so much smaller.

It was not until last fall, more than twenty years later, that our family decided to rebuild. But when Grandpa informed the neighbor, he insisted he did not remember making such an agreement. Moreover, he immediately put up his own wall on his side of our wall to prove his point. Which is how we came to have a double wall.

How do I know so much about such ancient history? I heard it from my mother. For the past several months, every time I wandered into the kitchen to peer into the fridge or sat down to watch TV, she would grab me and start talking about it. I suppose she must have been desperate to talk to someone. Almost every day after work she went from one lawyer to another, but they all told her the same thing: "There is nothing you can do about it now." Or: "Why didn't you draw up a proper document in the first place?" Coming home late and exhausted, she and my father began to fight. Then Grandpa started taking long walks by himself and my father stopped coming home.

"Couldn't you just pretend that our land has always been this size?" I suggested once, but my mother's expression made me wish that I hadn't.

"Are you actually trying to tell me that that would make it all right after we have been tricked and lied to like this?"

I could not answer. Her anger frightened me too much.

And besides, I didn't want to hear any more about it. After all, it was their problem, not mine. A grownup problem. I began to stay in my room studying in order to avoid my mother, but I couldn't concentrate. At those times, I really envied Tetsu. Adults never tried to talk to him about their problems. No, not to Tetsu, still so small and unreliable, incapable even of dressing himself properly, although he will start fourth grade next month.

But Tetsu has heard everything.

"Once I asked Grandpa, 'Why are you letting him get away with it? A creep like that deserves to die,' " Tetsu continues.

Not in my wildest dreams have I ever imagined that Tetsu would say something like that to Grandpa. "And what did he say?"

"He gave me a very serious look and told me I shouldn't think things like that." Tetsu huddles under the clothesline, looking cold. "Personally, I wouldn't mind if our house stayed just the way it is."

There is nothing I can say. In the light of the moon, the wall looms white, and perhaps because it is so bright, the darkness beyond appears even deeper, as if it is listening to us with bated breath.

. . .

The next day, Tetsu comes down with a fever. He shouldn't have stayed out in the rain without an umbrella all day, keeping watch on the next-door neighbor.

"He's a real villain, that old man," Tetsu groans, tormented by feverish dreams. "He burned it with the garbage."

Of course, I realize immediately that he means the cat. The next-door neighbor has a small silver-colored incinerator in which he burns their household garbage. His face, deeply lined and tanned from working in the garden, floats into my mind. That old man probably burns everything. Not just cats. He might even murder someone and then chop him up and burn him, too. For sure he could.

"And I thought he might have a heart attack or something." Tetsu tosses fitfully.

"He must have been surprised at least!"

"That's what you think. He just got mad and started yelling at his wife."

Suddenly I am very busy, buying medicine, making sure Tetsu takes it, changing his ice packs, warming up milk for him to drink. I feel compelled to do these things, because, unfortunately for me, I know his secret. Despite the fact that I have been trying so hard to ignore anything unpleasant.

"Tomomi?" Tetsu's voice is pitifully feeble and I peer into his bed. "I had a terrible nightmare." His eyes are half-closed. "I couldn't play the harmonica properly and a space alien killed me."

"It's your fever," I say.

"The music teacher, Miss Shiiki, was there. She's an alien, too."

The music teacher is pretty scary all right. She is very old.

"Miss Shiiki." Tetsu is racked with coughs and he fixes his eyes on mine as if he's about to make his dying request. "She wears a wig."

"How do you know?"

"It came off."

"Her wig?"

"Yes. You know, when we stand at attention and bow to the teacher at the beginning of the class? It fell off. *Plop.*" He does not even smile.

"You mean in your dream?" This is beginning to get ridiculous.

"No, no. I really saw it. When it slipped off, her head was covered in short bristles, just like the man's at the fish shop, completely white."

Then he whispers, his face solemn, "It was petrifying." His fever must still be fairly high.

"Why don't you rest? I'll wake you when it's suppertime."

"Mmm." Then he murmurs, "It's true, you know. About the music teacher," and falls asleep.

He is breathing peacefully, his cheeks flushed pink. It seems rather unfair. He is the one who chose to stand in the rain. He is the one who got a fever and made work for me. If it had been me, I certainly would not have stood out in the rain all day like that. Which is why I haven't come down with a fever.

When Tetsu was younger, he had allergies that made his skin dry and scaly, and he would wake Grandma up in the middle of the night, crying out, "I'm itchy! Itchy!" He kept her very busy. My mother started working after Tetsu was born, so he was really more like a child to Grandma than a grandchild. Every night he called out for her, weeping and wailing. Not for our mother but for Grandma, which is why she never got enough sleep.

When she died, I thought that she might have lived longer if Tetsu hadn't made her work so hard. Sometimes even now, when Tetsu gets on my nerves, I want to believe that. But it's not the truth. It's not his fault that she died.

Last winter was warm. I remember the cherry trees had already started to blossom by this time last year. Grandma was no longer able to urinate and fluid began to pool in her stomach. After the doctor warned us that she did not have long to live, she was in a coma for weeks, and the fluid in her stomach gradually pushed its way up, until, darkened by blood, it oozed from her mouth. My mother stayed at the hospital day after day, pushing gauze pads into her mouth to soak up the fluid that seeped out with a gurgling sound. For many days the wastebasket had been filled with pads stained deep red. Then I had the thought, "Grandma would be better off dead."

Although I did not want to think such a thing, although I had told her so many times that I wanted her to live forever, I went ahead and thought, "Grandma would be better off dead."

And the next day, at noon, she died. She died because of my thought. I never wanted her to die. I wanted her to be there always. Forever and ever, by my side. I know that my wish was sincere. But still she died.

That was when I began having nightmares about turning into a monster.

Sometimes I stare at Grandma's photograph. It's there on the family altar with candles and incense and pictures of other dead relatives. It's a smiling face, slightly out of focus. But it doesn't feel real to me. It doesn't seem like Grandma at all. When I try to remember her, the only image that comes to mind is her lying in the hospital with tubes coming out of her body, surrounded by big noisy machines. Someday I will probably suffer like that, too; suffer until the very end, and die. When I think about it, I feel that it would be much better if a nuclear bomb fell and wiped out the entire world instantly. I cannot remember Grandma very clearly. I am afraid to remember her.

Strangely enough, after Grandma died, Tetsu's allergies suddenly cleared up. Now Tetsu is sleeping with his cheek, so fair that it is hard to believe it was once dry and scaly, resting on top of a book opened facedown on the bed.

I slip the thick volume out from under him, and on the cracked and blackened binding it says *Ghosts from Around the World*. How can Tetsu read such things when he has a fever? There are plenty of other books that he likes, such as *An Introduction to Detection* or *The Secrets Series*. I close the book hastily and shove it onto the very top shelf where Tetsu can't reach it. After all, it was opened to a chapter called "Goblin Cats." I'm a little worried. Maybe Tetsu is thinking about the cat. Maybe his fever is the cat's curse.

But the next day his temperature is normal. I am sitting at my desk, peering into a mirror and cutting my bangs, when he gets up and begins to get dressed, his legs as pale and weak as long-stemmed mushrooms.

"You shouldn't get up yet. Remember what Mom said."

The bangs above my left eyebrow are shorter than the other side, so I try to even them out. But this time I cut the right side too short. My mother says I should go to the beauty parlor, but I hate going. I get so nervous sitting in front of an enormous mirror while the hairdresser stares at me. Once the hairdresser was a man and that was even worse. By the time he finished, my back was as stiff as a board and I tripped getting out of the chair and hit my head on the glass partition. So now I always cut my own bangs and let the back grow long; it has a wave that sometimes curls outward and sometimes in, but I don't mind it that way. Still gazing into the mirror, I venture to ask, "You want to go to the doctor?"

"No."

"Want me to make you some instant soup?"

"No."

"It's the kind you like, with egg in it."

"Not right now."

"Hmm." Hmm. Now I have nothing to do again. "Are you going somewhere?"

"Mmm."

"You aren't supposed to go out yet."

"All right, then, I'll go to the doctor."

"I'll come with you."

"Then I'm not going."

"Well, where are you going if you're not going there?"

In the frustration of repeatedly trying to straighten them, I've now chopped my bangs short to about the middle of my forehead. Before I realize it, the top of my desk is covered in fine clippings of hair. I close the compact mirror with a snap. Tetsu is turning in circles with his head stuck inside a sweater.

"What if you aren't allowed to go out today? Grandpa is bound to say no."

Tetsu's head pops out of the sweater and his eyes are bleary.

"It's on backward," I remark, and he ducks his head back inside. While he struggles, his shirt comes out of his pants, exposing his stomach. I nudge him in the back of the knee as he staggers about, and his legs crumple under him and he hits his head, still covered by the sweater, on the corner of the dresser.

"Cut it out!" he yelps.

I scramble down the stairs and go into the TV room. He doesn't have a speck of appreciation for all the trouble I went to for him. Well, that's the last time I take care of him when he's sick!

But in the evening when Grandpa asks, "Where's Tetsu?" I am a little worried. I fell asleep with the TV on and didn't even notice what time he had left. Tetsu is nothing but trouble, I grumble to myself, and then notice that Grandpa is looking at me with a strange expression. "What?" I ask.

"Your hair . . . did you cut it?"

If he thinks it looks funny, why doesn't he just say so?

"I'll go look for Tetsu," I say and, flinging on a scarf, dash out the door.

Three

Puffing out white clouds of breath, just as if it were mid-winter, I head for the local shrine. Of all the places Tetsu might go, that is the only one that comes to mind at the moment.

There are a lot of hills around our house. The school is over and down one hill and at the top of the next. The first hill is almost entirely covered with houses except for the Hachi-man shrine at the very top. It is such a small shrine that you wouldn't think anyone would go there to worship, and except at festival time the cracked wooden shutters are always closed. Surrounded by tall trees, it is a gloomy place even at midday. Our teacher has warned us not to go there because it is gen-erally deserted, but Tetsu and I cut through the shrine every morning on our way to school even though it's slightly out of our way.

The stone steps are thick with fallen camellia flowers. Walking carefully so as not to tread on the petals, I try to remember when they were in full bloom. But I can't. Even though I used to pass this way every day.

I stop to catch my breath and look behind me. I stare down to the bottom of the long steep flight of steps that stretches on and on. I balance on the tips of my toes at the edge of a step and try to resist for as long as I can the feeling that I will be sucked down. It is against the rules to close your eyes. Once Tetsu and I played this falling game, shrieking excitedly, "I'm going to fall! I'm going to fall!" until Tetsu actually did fall and roll down the steps. His face when he glares toward the bottom is always deadly pale, his whole body rigid like a bent nail, yet it is always I who say, "Let's stop."

Playing by myself, however, is not much fun. I leap up the last ten steps and catch sight of the back of Tetsu's head poking out from behind the wooden collection box in front of the shrine. He is humming to himself.

I'll surprise him, I think. I sneak closer, draw a deep breath, and then—my heart freezes.

Squatting down and leaning against the box, Tetsu is not wearing his pants or even his underwear. He sits there with his sweater on, his scarf still wrapped around his neck, humming merrily, naked from the waist down. Did the fever affect his brain?

"Oh! Tomomi." I am frozen to the spot, but Tetsu points to the branch of a tree where his underpants are hanging. Like

28

a zombie under hypnosis, I walk jerkily toward the tree and mechanically reach out my hand. His pants are sopping wet. Coming immediately to my senses, I let out a shriek.

"They're clean. I washed them," Tetsu protests as if the shrine is an obvious place to wash your underpants. "Aren't they dry yet?"

"You washed them *here*?"

"My slacks are okay." His slacks are draped casually over the head of a stone dog. One leg is inside out.

"Well, I hope nobody saw you."

"Nope. Just the lady from the bakery."

"That's somebody!"

Now I'm done for. Of all people, he had to meet Kuwano's mother. Kuwano will be going to the same junior high as I will, and he is sure to say something when school begins. I regret my failure in the entrance exams from the bottom of my heart.

"But I saw a snake."

"A snake?"

"It was a garter snake. I've seen them in my encyclopedia." Tetsu's eyes are blinking rapidly, as they always do when he is excited. "It must have come out of hibernation."

"What has that got to do with your underpants?"

"A lot. When I chased after the snake, I pooped in my pants," he says in a loud voice and then erupts with laughter as if he has just heard the funniest joke. "Poo-poo!"

"Tetsu!"

He looks at my face and mumbles hesitantly, "It was just a little. Don't tell Mom, okay? Besides, I already washed them."

29

He points to a large square stone trough with the words "sacred water" carved on it standing near the top of the steps. I stare blankly at it for about five seconds. I think of the people who will use this water to purify themselves before approaching the shrine, washing their hands in it, rinsing their mouths out with it. The dipper has long since disappeared, if there ever was one, and the stone trough filled with rainwater is green with moss. But still . . .

"Well, it's none of my business if the gods curse you."

Tetsu's calm is unruffled. "The god of this shrine won't mind."

What he means by that, I have no idea. "Let's go home. If you wait for them to dry, you'll be here all night."

"Okay." Tetsu walks with his bare bottom over to the tree, takes his sopping-wet underpants off the branch, and starts to put them on.

"Forget your underpants," I say, taking them from him and handing him his slacks. He takes the slacks, which I have carefully turned right side out, and for some reason turns them inside out again, then right again, takes his sneakers off unsteadily and puts his left foot into the right leg of the slacks. I pretend not to notice.

A camellia flower falls—*plop*—at the same time that Tetsu suddenly remarks, "It isn't easy to find cats, is it?"

"You were looking for cats?"

"Yeah." He finally gets his foot into the correct leg. "They say cats hide from people when it's time to die. That's why I thought this might be a good place . . ."

But I just say, "Your zipper's undone." Tetsu looks down and pulls up the zipper. He leaves it half an inch undone.

I decide to let the zipper go. "So you're going to do it again? Put another dead cat in the neighbor's yard?"

"Yes."

"It doesn't have to be a cat, does it? Why don't you try a dirty rubber boot or garbage or something?"

Tetsu shakes his head, indicating that that wouldn't be the same. "I told you, the old man hates cats. How about you? Which would make you feel worse, a dead cat or an old boot?"

"A dead cat."

He spreads out his hands at my reply, as though there is no need to add anything further. I shift his underpants to my other hand.

"But don't you feel sorry for the cat?"

"What about Mom, then?"

"Huh?"

"What about Mom? Have you no compassion for her?"

I start to reply, then stop. I never expected Tetsu to say something like that.

"If I was a grownup, I could become a policeman and arrest that creep. Then execute him. Do you know about the thirteenth step?"

"No."

"The condemned man has a noose around his neck. He walks up the steps, and on the thirteenth step it falls away, his neck breaks—'*Arghh!*'—and he dies."

"Hmm." The words "Have you no compassion for her?"

31

are still chasing around and around in my mind. I had thought that my mother was just a nuisance when she tried to talk to me, and here's Tetsu using the word "compassion."

"Or how about tying each arm and leg to a different horse and going to a crossroads. With a crack of the whip, the four horses charge off in four different directions and *rrripp!* he's torn to pieces. Fantastic!" Tetsu yells, *"Rrripp!"* once more and then hums a cartoon theme song with such vigor that his head bobs up and down. He even adds background music to his stories. I heave a sigh of exasperation.

"It's true. They really do execute people that way in some countries. I read it in a book."

"But that was a long time ago, right?"

"Well, yeah."

"You've been reading too many weird books."

Tetsu tilts his head. His nostrils are flared.

"What?" I ask.

"You wouldn't understand."

"I wouldn't?"

"That's okay, though. It doesn't matter if you don't understand."

Slightly irritated, I speak in a sharp, demanding tone. "What is this, going on about thirteen steps and that kind of stuff? You're not making any sense."

"I told you, if I was a grownup—"

"Grownups can't do those things either," I snap, and Tetsu falls silent. He is drawing lines in the dirt with the toe of his sneaker. When he finishes drawing the seventh line, he says,

"I don't care if I die from a cat's curse." He says this like someone who has already resigned himself to that fate.

He snatches his underpants away from me and starts walking with them dangling from one hand. He picks up a fallen camellia flower, sucks the nectar, and walks down the steps, halting frequently. As I watch his receding back, he looks just the same as always, as if he has not changed a bit.

I am awakened at dawn by the sound of Tetsu grinding his teeth. I get up slowly and go downstairs. My father's shoes, which were at the back door yesterday, are gone. He must have left in the middle of the night.

Last night was awful, even though it was the first time we'd had supper together as a family for a long time. It was my father's fault. "Look," he said, "if living here is this much trouble, wouldn't it be better to move somewhere where the water and air are cleaner?" You'd think that he'd have more sense. To casually come home and then say something like that, in front of everyone, was guaranteed to make Mom furious. The discussion became increasingly complicated and they began to fight. Mom burst into tears, saying "It isn't fair!" and my father got flustered and hit her. I hoped that Grandpa would do something, but he retreated, announcing that he was going to bed. And then he went and started sorting out the storage room.

My father's shoes are not at the front door, either. I check the shoe cupboard where we put our shoes when we come inside. I kneel there, right beside the front door, and open the cupboard door softly, but then feel like a fool. I know they're not there, and yet here I am, stealthily opening the cupboard in my own house. I close it with a bang and the solitary sound is absorbed by the house where everyone else is still sleeping. My head hurts a little.

I go into the kitchen and warm some milk, standing on tiptoe on the cold floor. The opaque glass of the window is dyed blue like the ocean floor. "The sun is rising much earlier now," I think. "The blue glass is very beautiful." But I feel as if the person thinking those thoughts is someone else, not really me. And when I try to identify what I am actually thinking, I feel my headache growing worse. I give up and decide to let this stranger think whatever she wants.

"Do you remember, Tomomi?" The stranger is addressing me. "When we were little we often dreamed. A dream that this house was in water as blue and beautiful as this."

Yes, I remember.

"You swam about, opening the refrigerator or eating your meals, or lay floating on the bed, reading a book. Your mother was like the little mermaid princess in the fairy tale, with her hair swaying gently in the water. Your mother and father, grandmother and grandfather, and even baby Tetsu held hands and sang as you slowly danced. The song melted in the water with the foam and became the fragrance of sunshine. You floated gently up to the ceiling to change the light bulbs. It was beautiful when the bright light suddenly flashed through the water."

A slight film forms on the milk and I hurriedly turn off the burner. The stranger vanishes in the same instant.

"Goodbye," I whisper. "Goodbye."

I quietly climb the stairs and huddle in bed as I drink my warm milk. I would like to have that dream again, I think, but I can't sleep a wink.

Four

Although I certainly didn't plan to, later that day I go with Tetsu to look for cats. Or, more accurately, for dead cats. I am sure that we will never find any, and to tell the truth I have no idea what I would do if we did. It's just that I am sick of staying home.

This morning I lay in bed for a while staring at the stained ceiling, as if I had only become aware for the first time of how decrepit our house is. Other families would have rebuilt their house years ago, before it got to the state ours is in. Modern houses are built using materials that can't withstand the hot and humid climate, and aren't meant to last very long, so it's not uncommon for families to demolish and rebuild their houses on the same lot after only twenty or thirty years have passed. But for some reason, we have waited until our house is falling apart. It is old, leaky, and full of drafts. Its floorboards are swollen in places as if they have absorbed decades' worth of damp, the wooden storm doors stick, and the bath tiles are full of cracks. It is a complete dump, both inside and out. I hate it. I detest this ramshackle house in which we are miserably squabbling over a few square yards of land with a single cherry tree growing on it.

"It's a secret. Don't tell Mom, or Grandpa either." Tetsu, who is fumbling with his shoes in the hallway, looks at me with round eyes when he realizes I intend to accompany him.

"What do you mean? I didn't tell them about the poop incident, did I?"

Tetsu hunches his shoulders like a bird on a telephone wire. "Tomomi."

"Yeah?"

"Why did you cut your hair?"

I press my bangs flat with the palm of my hand. The jagged edges prickle my forehead. "It's a little late to ask me that now."

"But I just noticed now."

I yank his ear as hard as I can and go outside.

The old man next door is gardening again. He is standing on a stepladder, trimming the hedge. The trees next door are always so neatly trimmed it makes me think the old man must watch them constantly, making sure that not a twig is allowed to grow even half an inch longer.

He reaches out precariously and clips a high branch. When his wife, who is watching anxiously from the doorway, tells him to be careful, he barks out in a voice like a distorted radio, "Water!" The old woman disappears hurriedly into the house, gets a glass of water, and holds it up to him from the bottom of the ladder. But he yells furiously, "What are you doing? A *bucket* of water! A bucket!" and the old woman hastily retreats back into the house.

"If only he would fall off that ladder," I say, looking around at Tetsu. But he just says, "Hurry up. Let's go," and turns his back on the neighbor. Then he sets off, looking up briefly at the weak white light of the sun as if to determine his direction.

"Fall, fall, fall," I chant silently to myself. But the old man does not fall off the ladder or even notice that I'm staring at him. My chest begins to feel heavy inside, as if it is full of water.

"Tetsu, wait!" I run after him to catch up.

He walks in silence straight down the road behind the technical high school, cuts through the parking lot of an apartment building, and turns down several narrow streets that pass through a residential area. He is terribly pigeon-toed and his stride is far from smooth, but his pace is surprisingly swift. Just trying to keep up with him, I have become hot all over and my skin prickles with sweat.

The scent of trees and grass is carried on the wind. I stretch my back and draw the air deep into my lungs. This scent is the same one that accompanies spring each year. Last year, the year before, and the year before that, I must have smelled it and liked it. So why is it that this year, enveloped within the same fragrance, I feel as though I have forgotten to do something very important while time has swiftly passed me by? It's like wearing a skirt that is too small or a blouse with a tight collar. I feel constricted and uncomfortable.

When we pass the sports arena, which I have previously only seen from a distance, I lose all sense of direction. We turn down a road where a solitary tofu shop sits surrounded by ordinary houses, and suddenly we come out at the top of a steep hill. How can that be when I have no recollection of climbing uphill? We must have been climbing gradually without my noticing it.

"Do you know where we are?" I am a little anxious. But Tetsu just turns for an instant, grunting, "Huh?" and begins trotting down the hill. Before he started elementary school, Grandma took him to the ear doctor several times. But the doctor kept telling her that there was nothing wrong with his ears. In the end, I think we just resigned ourselves to the fact that, although Tetsu can hear, he simply chooses not to listen.

As we walk, we draw ever closer to a metallic clanging sound, which I find upon reaching the bottom of the hill comes from within a building enclosed in rusted tin sheeting. The words *Yamamoto Recycling Center* are printed on a sign from which the paint has started to peel.

"What's this?"

"Don't you know?" Tetsu runs ahead with his neck craning forward and his rear end sticking out as usual. He pokes his head through a gap in the tin sheeting and peers about enthusiastically.

The first thing I see is something that looks like a round

disk suspended from a ceiling as high as that of a gymnasium. It begins to descend, swaying slowly, and a colorful block of metal is sucked into the air and clings to it. Looking more closely, I realize that the varicolored metal is actually crushed soda cans.

"It's a giant magnet. Amazing, isn't it?" Tetsu exclaims, still leaning forward. "How many cans do you think there are in one block?"

"About a hundred, I guess." But I couldn't care less. It's just a scrap yard. What has it got to do with cats?

"No way. I bet there's a thousand."

The disk raises the block of cans and moves it to a place where similar blocks have already been piled up like giant caramels. There is a clang as it is dropped from the magnet and becomes part of that neat mound.

"I picked up some cans and brought them here the other day." Tetsu suddenly waves his hand. There is a small room with a glass window near the ceiling where someone must be controlling the movements of the magnet. A man with a big square face who is wearing a hard hat waves back.

"I'd sure like to operate that thing. I'm going to work here when I grow up."

"Let's go." Suddenly I am very tired. I have not slept well. "We haven't seen a single cat yet."

"You go on ahead, Tomomi," Tetsu says, gazing raptly at the ponderous movements of the disk. "I'm going to watch a little longer."

I squat down. I have no choice but to do it his way. Even if I did go on home, he wouldn't leave now. It was he who decided to do this in the first place, and besides, I can't remember the way home.

There is no way I am going to keep Tetsu company in such foolishness again.

"It's very noisy," I think, but then realize that it's folk dance music. Everyone is dancing in the gym. I am in a circle with my school friends, my teachers, even my friends from the cram school. Everyone is wearing pretty clothes and smiling. The music becomes louder and louder and I whirl about, transported. I feel as light as a bird, thinking that I have never done anything so well. I am sure everyone must be thinking how beautiful I look, that I am a dance star.

But at that moment, I get a shock. I am the only one wearing no clothes. I am dancing in the nude. I look around, wondering what to do, but no one seems to have noticed yet. Just when I am about to sneak away, a boy with a leering face appears right in front of me and says, "You're naked and you'll be naked for the rest of your life."

I wake up. What a lousy dream. It's still dark outside and there is no sound.

I consider getting up to go to the toilet but instead I lie there and become wide awake. I know that leering face. Of all people, why did it have to be that boy?

It was over a year ago, in gym class. The teacher was that disgusting Mr. Noguchi, as usual. Our class had been divided into groups for a relay race and I was on the same team as the leering boy. When a girl with a bad leg was assigned to our group, he said something really mean to her. "There isn't any point in trying with you on our team." I was the only one who heard what he said, other than the girl with the bad leg, because he said it right into her ear.

I made a grab for him, and when he sidestepped, I chased him around the gym. I was so upset that I completely lost my head. All I remember is that I bit Mr. Noguchi on the arm when he tried to stop me. Mr. Noguchi let out a short squeal and then slapped me.

I had to stand for the rest of the class and recess, too, because I refused to explain or apologize. During recess, the girl with the bad leg didn't come to see me but the boy did. With a smirk on his face, he announced, "Mr. Noguchi told Mrs. Saeki." Mrs. Saeki was my homeroom teacher. "He said you were emotionally unstable."

That night I felt so ashamed and furious I wept under my covers. I wished my body were a bomb and would explode into a million pieces.

But now I can't even weep the way I did then. Helpless, I can only stand mute and watch my family fall apart. But it is hard. Excruciatingly hard. I didn't realize until now how much pain I've been in.

Kacha, kacha, kacha . . . I listen to Tetsu grinding his teeth. Tetsu. He's probably right, I think. If we were grownups, we could find some other way. I could leave home and maybe even forget my mother, my father, everyone. But if all we can do right now is search for dead cats, then I will go again tomorrow. And with that thought, the turmoil in my heart is somewhat eased.

I close my eyes and don't open them again until morning.

. . .

I follow along behind Tetsu all day like an oversized duckling. When he visits the recycling center, I gaze at the crushed metal with him. When, for some unfathomable reason, he squeezes himself through the narrow space between a wall and a telephone pole, I do the same. When he pokes his head into an opening in a drainpipe, I do, too. Tetsu shouts into the darkness, "*O-y!*" His voice echoing in the empty pipe sounds funny, so I try it, too. "*Oy! Oy!*" we bellow repeatedly, and then suddenly we both burst out laughing. Our laughter collides in the dark drainpipe, until it sounds as if it's filled with strange little creatures from some unknown land far away.

We walk to the elementary school and climb over the gate. When he first started to climb over it, I told him not to. It seemed like trespassing, and the school, hushed and aloof in spring break, turned a cold, indifferent face to me.

We pass along behind the wall of the gymnasium, wading through old gym mats and scraps of wood, and finally emerge at a tiny swamp. Ivy twines thickly around the trees surrounding it, and the ferns that poke out from under a deep layer of fallen leaves are a vivid green from last night's rain.

"I never knew this was here," I exclaim, and Tetsu beams, blinking his eyes.

"It's called Reed Marsh," he says. He throws a pebble into the pond and the water, green with algae, makes a ring, smooth like jelly, framing our reflections. "Soon there will be lots of frogs' eggs to collect."

"Do you come here often?"

"Uh-huh."

"I wish I had known about it before I graduated."

"You could still come. On vacation, like today."

"And climb over that gate every time?"

"Why not?"

But I know it wouldn't be the same now that I'd graduated.

Tree branches cover the sky, resembling the poster of the human circulatory system in our science class. It seems strange that our veins and arteries should resemble tree branches. If the tree branches are veins, then is the sky skin?

At noon we return home and eat the noodles Grandpa has prepared. During lunch, Tetsu suggests that we go down to the river.

"Okay," I reply, then steal a quick glance at Grandpa. Tetsu looks a bit guilty. I am waiting for Grandpa to ask us why we go out walking every day, but he just eats his noodles silently. Tetsu and I look at each other with relief. Grandpa is still busy tidying up the storage room and neither of us wants to stay home with him.

When we reach the river embankment, the sky suddenly seems enormous. The river plain stretches off forever, curving gently like a belt fringed with the faint green of a baseball diamond and a soccer field. We head down the side of the embankment, cut across the field, and follow a path through the tall dry grasses to where the river slowly glides along, carrying the glittering sunlight.

"You know the Yangtze?" Tetsu asks.

"It's the name of a river, isn't it?"

"Do you know what country it's in?"

"China."

He blinks at me as if impressed by my knowledge. "There are eels there. Eels bigger than a man."

"Hmmm." Tetsu never eats eel. The only things he will eat without complaining are noodles and custard.

He stares into the water as if looking for something. I sit down on the grass. As I relax, caressed by the river breeze, I am suddenly overcome by the strange feeling that I don't exist, that my lying here soaking up the sunlight is unreal, and I'm filled with a restless uneasiness. This river flowed here before I was born and will doubtless continue to do so after I die. I am just a small insignificant dot. I can't change anything, I cannot achieve anything. No matter what thoughts I think, not even a single speck of star dust will ever respond.

I don't think that my father will come back this time. This one simple thought torments me so much that I can't bear it. Yet not even the old man next door, let alone the universe, gives a damn. I press my arms firmly against my chest and rest my forehead gently on my bent knees. Something within me is screaming to be let out.

What if we do find another dead cat? To be honest, I don't want to find one. If we did, what would be the right thing to do with it? Should we throw it into the neighbor's yard? Should we make a grave and bury it? Should I just pretend not to see it? I have no idea. But one thing is certain. A small, stiff cat corpse is inexorably creeping up on us, demanding to know, "What are you going to do with me?"

"Tomomi! Come over here!" Tetsu is up to his ankles in the water. "Take off your socks but put your shoes back on so you won't cut your feet."

"It's too cold," I say.

Tetsu peers into the water as if following something, wipes his nose on his sleeve, and starts throwing pebbles into the river. The light on the river's surface is gradually turning a honey color and the water seems heavier and thicker.

"You'd better get out."

When he comes out of the water, his feet and ankles are so cold it looks as if he's wearing pink socks. I take off my sweat-shirt and wipe his feet, and then rub them over and over with the palms of my hands. While I rub them, I try to remember Grandma. When Tetsu was younger he was thin and bony, a weak little child always falling down. Every evening Grandma put his feet in hot and then cold water, massaging them, and saying, "Grow strong, grow strong," like an incantation. I try to remember what she looked like then, but all I can remember is how much I envied Tetsu.

"That tickles," Tetsu complains, but he stays still.

Grow strong, grow strong. But I don't know what it means to be strong.

"Okay. You're done!" I give Tetsu's knees a slap.

Five

I meet the woman that evening on our way home.

As Tetsu and I stroll along the embankment together, someone comes huffing and puffing up the steep slope, pushing a bicycle. The front basket is filled with dishpans and plastic containers from the deli counter of a supermarket, and the rear basket holds a bucket.

"Oh!" she cries out with pleasure, looking in our direction.

I turn to look behind me. There is only a crow playing with a discarded wrapper that is being tossed lightly by the wind.

"Ah!" Tetsu exclaims, blinking. I grab his arm tightly. This woman is weird. Although it is not yet summer, she is wearing a broad-rimmed flower-print hat tied with a ribbon. The pants of her baggy sweatsuit are almost worn through at the knees and are covered in fuzz balls. If it weren't for the hat, I might have mistaken her for a man because of her square face, which lacks any trace of makeup. Her voice is deep and hoarse, too.

"It's you!" she exclaims, huskily.

"Yup!" Tetsu replies, grinning. His cheeks have a faint pink blush, as if he is meeting a cute girl that he has a crush on. While I stand there wondering what on earth is going on, he runs behind her bike and begins pushing it, grunting with the effort. Stunned, I merely watch the bicycle laden with junk make its way to the top of the embankment.

"Thank you so much! You're a great help." The woman beams, dripping with sweat. She is smiling at me, even though I didn't help, and when she says, "You his sister?" I mumble yes. I am not comfortable with gregarious people.

"She's the operator. You know, the one at the recycling place," Tetsu explains. I see. So she controls the magnet, does she? But I thought . . .

"You thought I was a man, didn't you?"

"Yes," I answer without thinking, and she laughs uproariously, startling me. But her laugh is generous.

"People often tell me I look like a plump, effeminate middle-aged man." It sounds very complicated.

"Is it hard to operate that thing?" Tetsu asks, and the woman grins broadly. There is a gold cap on one of her front teeth.

"Not a bit," she says.

Tetsu seems transfixed by that big gold tooth, but then,

hopping up and down, he peers into the bucket on the back of the bicycle. "Tomomi! Tomomi! Look at this. Come here!"

The woman is nodding as if to say, "Go ahead. Take a look."

The bucket is filled to the brim with a mess of stewed cabbage and dried fish. "What is this?" I blurt out, looking at the woman's face.

"Tonight's dinner," she replies, and begins pushing her bicycle along the embankment. Tetsu follows after her.

"Tetsu, I'm going home."

"Go ahead," he says without even glancing my way.

"Are you sure that's all right?" the woman asks, looking back at him.

"Sure, no problem!" Tetsu responds brightly.

But I can't just leave him there.

Refrigerators, TV sets, beds with no legs, electric fans, heaters, juicers, toilet bowls, bicycles, and unidentifiable objects of various kinds . . . past the tennis courts and the driving school, we discover all kinds of junk down along the bottom of the embankment, on the side away from the river. Although situated at the foot of giant concrete pillars supporting the expressway and enveloped by the roar of car engines, the spot seems somehow lonely and deserted.

When the woman bangs on an aluminum dishpan with a scoop, a single black cat slips slowly out of a rust-encrusted minibus.

"Tomomi, look!"

Cats appear from the shadow of a fridge, from behind a

broken shoe cupboard, one by one, seemingly without end. The numbers are unbelievable. The woman scoops the cabbage and dried fish stew from the bucket and fills the dishpans and plastic containers.

"Can I help?" Tetsu asks.

"Sure," the woman says, handing him a container.

Tetsu carries it over to the cats and places it gently on the ground. The cats, who have been watching his unfamiliar face cautiously, rush toward the food as soon as he backs away, and begin to eat.

"Here you go." I am gazing absently at the scene when the woman plunks a dishpan, heavy as stone, in my hands.

"B-but—" I never said that I wanted to help . . .

"Over there, over there," she says to me, pointing. The cats, their noses quivering in anticipation, come toward me. They're somewhat frightening.

When I go to place the dishpan on the tin sheet the woman is indicating, the cats pounce on it and I snatch my hands away. It would be a fine mess if they ate my hands, too.

Tetsu and I are so busy distributing food to the cats like caterers at a dinner party that when the bucket is finally empty we can only stare vacantly at the incredible scene. There are about thirty cats altogether.

"I didn't know that cats ate cabbage," Tetsu says, fascinated. "I need to read a more detailed book about them."

"Cats often chew weeds and grass, although many turn up their noses at lemons and shiitake mushrooms." The woman takes off her flower-print hat and wipes her forehead with the towel that hangs around her neck. Her short hair is permed in tight curls. She does look like a man.

"They eat grass?" Tetsu queries.

"Sure do. Dogs, cats, people, too. We all need to eat our vegetables," she intones solemnly in her gravelly voice. Tetsu hates vegetables, so he ignores this remark. "Well, I'm so glad you came along. It was much easier with you helping." She begins gathering the empty containers. Every single one is shiny and spotless, truly licked clean. The cats, having finished their meal, are busy licking themselves now.

"Do you feed the cats every day?" I ask, placing a bowl in the basket.

"Yup, twice a day. Morning and evening."

"Why?"

"Why?" She laughs. "I wonder, now. Why do I?" And she puts her hat back on.

She lives in a rickety wooden apartment building. We climb up the iron staircase and see a green washing machine that looks even older than the apartment building, its paint faded by the sun.

"I'm going home," I say for what must be the fifth time, tugging on Tetsu's shirt tail, which is hanging out of his slacks. He just says, "Huh? What?" barely glancing back before plowing on after the woman.

The door opens onto the kitchen, where a huge aluminum pot perches precariously on top of a gas burner. It is still half-filled with cabbage and dried fish stew.

"Are you sure you shouldn't be going home now? It's already six o'clock," the woman says.

"Nobody's home anyway," Tetsu replies, clumsily scooping the cabbage slop from the pot that the woman is holding into the bucket.

"What about your mother?"

"She's dead."

"Oh, really?" The woman looks at Tetsu as if to say, "You poor thing." I squeeze my eyes shut, afraid that they may pop out of my head.

"Where are you going now?" Tetsu asks. He is so excited that his spiky hair is practically standing on end.

"The park."

"The one with the pond?"

"Yup. Behind the boathouse."

"Are there lots of cats there?"

"Enough to sell."

"You . . ."

"What?"

"You sell cats?"

She barks with laughter again. "If I did, I would be very rich."

Tetsu looks stunned. "Are you rich?"

I am embarrassed, but she is laughing so hard I can almost see down her throat. Suddenly she notices me and covers her mouth with her hand as if to hide her fillings. It's a little late to remember your manners now, I think.

"What's wrong, Tomomi?" Tetsu demands.

"Nothing."

"Come on. What is it?"

"You've lost your marbles," I say, shaking my head.

Tetsu looks down. I wonder if I have hurt his feelings but then notice that his eyes are roving searchingly about the floor. He's looking for his marbles.

The woman is struggling to suppress her laughter with her hands over her mouth. Her face is as red as the devil's. I think that mine must be, too.

More than seventeen cats have gathered behind the little boathouse in the park. I say seventeen but I don't really know how many there are. By the time I count the ones that are eating, they disappear, to be replaced by new cats until I can no longer keep track. The moon has already risen high in the sky when we finish dishing out the food, collect the containers, and say goodbye to the woman. Tetsu and I race through the soft, misty light.

"Mom will be home by now for sure." My voice is slightly anxious.

"Yeah, she should be. And she's going to be mad," Tetsu says calmly. He doesn't mind Mom's being angry. That's because he's used to it.

"Hey, Tetsu." I stop and wait for him. "Do you think that lady is married?" He looks at me in surprise. "I don't think so," I continue, running along beside him.

"Why?"

"Did you see the room on the other side of the kitchen?

53

There was a dresser, a TV, and a little folding table. That was it. And the fridge was really small." My breath comes in gasps because I am running and talking at the same time.

"You noticed an awful lot," he says, drawing his eyebrows together in a frown.

"What's wrong with that?"

"You shouldn't do that. Grandma always said not to stare at things in other people's houses."

"I wasn't staring!" I snap and speed up suddenly, annoyed with him. "You should talk! You conveniently killed off our mother!"

I like running at full speed because you can hear your own footsteps following you. The sound of my feet at first rains down on top of my head, then falls back to explode from far behind me, and I feel like running harder to get farther and farther away from it. But the sound of my sneakers on the asphalt becomes louder and I stop, gasping.

Resting both hands on my knees, I pant like a dog. Feeling the pounding of my heart with my whole body, I make a fist with one hand. I learned in school that a person's heart is the same size as their fist. As I stare at it, I think that no matter how far I go, no matter how many things I see in my life, I will never see my heart with my own eyes. The idea that something I have never seen is keeping me alive and causing me to move gives me the shakes. When I think of that, I want to run. Like now.

Looking back, I see Tetsu's white face in the glow of a streetlamp as he comes up from behind, bobbing up and down along the night road. He runs right by me without stopping, wavering unsteadily like a ghost.

"Hey! And to think I waited for you!" This time we don't stop running until we reach home.

I look as if someone is pressing the barrel of a shotgun against my back. It is the group photo of our school trip in the graduation album. Everyone else is laughing, or has been caught with eyes closed. I look so stupid, the only one with such a solemn expression. In the photo of our first day in the school swimming pool, my bathing cap is too tight, pulling one eye up, while in the photo of our class play, I am right smack in the middle of the stage standing straight and tall but facing in the wrong direction. I knew I should never have looked at this album. Just one glance at it on graduation day was enough for me to know that I would hate it.

But, tossing and turning in the cool blue light of dawn, I'm afraid the dream I just had is going to come back. It is growing lighter outside and the squeal of the newspaper delivery man's bicycle brakes comes closer. I don't think I could sleep, even if I tried.

In my dream, I was in a pure white room. I didn't know where on earth I was. The walls, all white, began to revolve around me like a roulette wheel, circling faster and faster until a wind sprang up. Then, suddenly, they stopped moving as though someone had commanded them to. In front of me was a mirror, black like the bottom of a pond. I peered into it, squinting, and could see some shape trying to float upward, slowly swaying. I felt, without reason, that it must be something horrible, a monster . . .

I heave a small sigh, relieved that I woke up.

The sound of bicycle brakes grows suddenly louder and the lid of our mailbox clangs. The newspaper. Perhaps I should go get it. But it's probably freezing outside. I hunch down under the covers and bite the nails on my right hand, and flip the pages of the album with my left by the light of my bedside lamp. Under the heading "All Together," a page filled with small snapshots, I find a picture that I hadn't noticed before.

It is a photo from when I was in fourth grade, of four girls standing in the school yard. I am standing on the far left with my hand slightly raised and my neck stretched out as if I am calling to the person behind the camera.

I suddenly feel just as I did when I smelled spring on the wind the other day. I was not so tall or slim when this picture was taken. My eyes and face were perfectly round. I didn't worry about my bangs all the time, pulling at them or cutting them, nor was I in the habit of chewing my fingernails. I often went to the pool with my friends. I think I was nicer then. I never thought unkind things about others, or lied, or had secrets. And I didn't dream about monsters.

But the greatest difference is that when this picture was taken it was easy for me to imagine what I would be like when I grew up. I could see myself, scarf blowing in the wind, clutching a book in some foreign language, waving goodbye before getting on a plane. Or racing in my sportscar to rescue people from some terrible disaster, arriving gallantly on the scene just in time to save the day. Or standing before a grand piano as large as a ship and bowing gracefully to the audience. Or wearing a wedding dress.

All of these dreams seem ridiculous now. I can't believe I had such romantic images of how my life would be. But when I try to imagine what kind of person I will be when I grow up, nothing comes to mind at all except myself grown taller. I have been carefully avoiding milk and am trying to squeeze my feet into shoes that are too tight. Even so, my skirt grows shorter and shorter and my feet are wearing holes in the toes of my shoes. I feel as if my body has been taken over by an alien, and I am powerless to stop the changes that are happening.

If only it were possible not to grow up. That would be infinitely preferable. Grownups are always fighting. They fight, get sick, and then, like Grandma, they suffer and die.

But whenever I think such thoughts, I am overcome with a terrible loneliness, like a monster wailing all alone. I close the album with a snap and push it under the mattress.

The old man next door is spraying pesticide. Wearing rubber gloves and a mask, he pours poison diluted with water into the metal container of a sprayer. Then he drenches not only the trees, which have been trimmed ruler-straight, but the whole garden. The awful stench steals in through the kitchen window and permeates our noses, our mouths, even our stomachs as we eat our lunch.

"He's spraying again! One of these days he's going to kill his own trees with that stuff," I remark.

Grandpa says nothing. Tetsu is biting the tips of his chopsticks. I stand up to close the window. It's warped and won't close properly, so I open it wide and shut it with a bang. Even then, it's still open a crack at the bottom.

"Close it more quietly, can't you?" Grandpa says, without looking up from his bowl of noodles.

"But it doesn't shut all the way."

After lunch, Grandpa takes a candle stub from a drawer and begins rubbing it along the window frame. Opening and closing the rickety window, he checks how it glides. I can't bear to stick around any longer.

Going out onto the narrow porch, I look at the garden strewn with old flowerpots and planters, and I find it already covered in weeds. Little green shoots are poking their heads through the soil around the roots of the azalea and the Japanese laurel, even through the cracks in the concrete.

"Last year's tulips are coming up!" I call out to Grandpa from the porch, but it is Tetsu, not Grandpa, who slides open the door.

"Can't smell them from here," he says, wrinkling his nose and sniffing. Of course he can't. Tulips have no scent. "Tomomi, let's go there again."

"Where?"

"The place with the broken bus."

"You mean that garbage dump we were at yesterday?"

"Yeah."

I am not too keen on the idea. The cats all had pus running from their eyes and were terribly thin. They looked so miserable it was depressing. Cats are supposed to hide when it is time to die, but what am I going to do if one drops dead in

58

front of me? That would be even worse than finding one that is dead already.

Just then we hear something sliding across the thick woven straw of the tatami-mat floor. Grandpa, his paunch sticking out, is half carrying, half dragging the old organ. Tetsu and I hurry to push the doors open wide and Grandpa sets it down on the porch, grunting. He takes a deep breath but immediately starts coughing. His face is bright red. With his high blood pressure, I wish he wouldn't overdo it like this.

"What are you going to do with it?"

He doesn't answer because, although his coughing has ceased, he is busy lighting another cigarette.

"You going to fix it?"

He finally nods in reply. My first thought is "Not again!" Grandpa is back to his "We can still use it" theme.

He always insists on repairing things, saying that they can still be used. When the door fell off the refrigerator, we all thought it was finally time to buy a new one. After all, it was ancient and the metal hinge holding the door had broken in half. But he worked on it for two whole days and fixed it. There is a little trick to closing it, but we are still using that old wreck. The TV in his room is the same. It dates back to before I was born, and every time it stops working, Grandpa fixes it. Even when it's fixed, he can get only two channels. Once my mother decided to buy him a new one as a present, but he flatly refused to accept it, saying, "No matter how many channels it has, you can only watch one channel at a time, so this one is good enough for me." But he still occasionally peers at the back of the set, trying to figure out how to get the channels with the historical dramas he likes. At those times, my mother sighs, "I don't know whether he's stubborn or just a sore loser."

"Wow!" Tetsu shouts, dancing around the organ. The board at the back is completely covered in green mold.

Totally unconcerned, Grandpa, puffing out smoke, stands alongside the broken organ, which is bathed in sunlight for the first time in decades. They look like old buddies.

"Aren't you two going out?"

"Do you need help?" I ask, just in case, but he says, "No, thanks."

We leave.

"That lady will come again today, won't she?" Tetsu asks.

"She should. She said she comes every day." So Tetsu is still planning to go where the ragged old cats live. I sigh.

"What is Grandpa going to do with that old organ once he fixes it, anyway?" he says, kicking a banana peel that has been squashed by a car.

I shrug my shoulders. Who knows?

Six

Tetsu runs past pieces of sheet metal, a refrigerator lying on its side, and a bicycle without wheels, chasing after cats. Although it would be more accurate to say that he is chasing cats away. No matter how much he insists, "I won't hurt you. Honestly, I won't," whenever he gets close they all dart off, slipping into the tiniest crevices. I sit down on an old microwave oven perched at the highest point of the junk heap and point, saying, "Look! There's one," or "It ran over here."

"You're doing it wrong," I finally say. "It's driving me crazy!"

"Well, why don't you try it, then?"

"Watch how it's done," I boast, but before I know it I am drenched with sweat. Not only am I unable to catch any cats, I can't even manage to touch the tip of a tail. "Stupid cats! If I do catch any of you, I'll make mincemeat out of you!"

"Tomomi, stop! You're scaring them! Sit down!" Tetsu screeches.

"Hey!" A strange man is waving to us from the top of the embankment. His voice reaches us in snatches, blown away by the river wind, which is growing stronger. ". . . dangerous . . . shouldn't . . ."

"We're in trouble now," I think, and in that moment of distraction, the black-and-white cat I'm about to grab dives beneath a washing machine, swinging its tail. I click my tongue in disgust. I had almost caught it.

". . . throw garbage . . . there . . ." The man continues, totally misunderstanding the situation.

"The cat ran away!" I yell back in exasperation, and he walks off, shaking his head.

Suddenly I realize that I can no longer hear the sound of Tetsu's feet on the sheets of metal or the hood of the bus. Where could he have gone?

"Tetsu!" I call. The wind dies down occasionally as if it has forgotten to blow, then starts up again with an even stronger gust. The sweat dries on my skin and I sneeze violently.

I find Tetsu asleep in the broken-down minibus. His cheek is pressed against the muddy seat and he breathes deeply. He must have been exhausted from all that running around. The cats usually sleep in the bus and it smells funny, so I open the window and spread my sweater over him.

Sitting on the seat looking out, I feel as though I have come a long way. The green grass of the embankment, the sky, the junk pile—framed by the bus window, they look so different from a moment ago. If only it were a magic bus that could ride to the bottom of the sea or through the middle of an active volcano. Looking through the window is a bit like looking into my mirror, and I start to doze off.

The woman shakes her head as she ladles out a stew of seaweed and half-dried fish. "It's strange," she says. "The cats seem rather shy today. Suspicious, or something."

"Maybe it's because the wind is so strong," Tetsu says, feigning innocence. The cats stare at him accusingly.

"Maybe that's it," she says, shaking her head again and then spitting on the ground. "It sure is an awful wind. It makes my mouth all gritty inside."

Tetsu draws his brows together, purses his lips like a clown, and grimaces. Then he sucks his cheeks in and out and spits on the ground—*splat*! His eyes blink with pleasure.

"Tetsu! Cut it out!" I glare at him. "That's disgusting!"

Tetsu and I squat down and watch the cats eat. Even while they're eating, the cats twitch their ears the whole time. Although they occasionally swat a neighbor lightly with a paw if he pushes too close, they never fight over their food. When they have finished, we stand up slowly to show that we have no intention of chasing them again, and gather up the dishpans.

"So cats eat seaweed," Tetsu says as he loads the dishpans and the bucket onto the woman's bicycle.

"Sure do," she responds.

"I've been thinking," Tetsu says, looking back at the cats, who are now licking themselves clean. "Cats like fish, right? Fish and seaweed both come from the sea. Maybe that's why they like seaweed."

"Could be," the woman says, seriously. "You're pretty smart, Tetsu."

"Naw, not really. Tomomi's smarter than me." But he is grinning like an idiot. "Well, explain why they eat cabbage, then, smarty-pants," I feel like saying, but decide against it.

We part from her halfway along the embankment. "Mom was mad at us for being so late yesterday," Tetsu explains, and the woman raises her eyebrows in surprise.

"Oh? So your mother's alive, is she?" She gives him a sideways glance, grinning slyly.

I flick his forehead with my finger to say I told you so.

"Ow!"

"Lying is the root of robbery," I chide him, quoting an old Japanese proverb.

"It's none of your business," he snaps. "I didn't lie to you. And besides, it's 'Lying is the *first step to* robbery.' "

"So you're not going to say you're sorry?"

But before a red-faced Tetsu can apologize, the woman is already saying, "Never mind," and patting him on the head. Only it is more like ruffling than patting, making his thin scraggly hair stand straight up.

"Hurry on home," she says. "It looks like rain."

Tetsu nods, and then asks, "What should you do if you want to make friends with a cat?"

"Hmmm." Her eyebrows leap apart like the opposing ends

of two magnets. "Well, you should never try to pick them up suddenly or chase after them."

"What should you do, then?" Tetsu's nostrils flare.

"They'll come to you in their own good time."

"When is that?"

"You have to get to know them, little by little. Little by little," she says, pulling her square jaw in on the word "little," her deep gravelly voice rumbling even deeper.

"How?" Tetsu demands.

"Like I said. Little by little. Gradually, you know."

"But when I try to touch them even a little, they just run away." Tetsu pulls his pale, pointed chin in on the word "little," too.

She looks at us as if to say "Aha!" I hastily shake my head in denial.

"Don't rush it. Cats hate children, carpenters, and vacuum cleaners. And adult cats and strays are especially cautious."

"Hmmm." Tetsu purses his lips again and says, "Okay!" and runs down the embankment.

"See you," the woman says, waving at me. I wave back as I climb down. I feel as if she is still watching me, and turn to look back. But she is moving away, pushing her bicycle slowly, lurching occasionally.

"Hey, Tomomi. She said carpenters and vacuum cleaners. Carpenters have hammers and it would hurt to be hit by one, so that makes sense. But why vacuum cleaners? Do you think it's because they would lose all their fur if they were sucked up inside one?" Tetsu trots along, looking back again and again, while he is talking.

At that moment I hear a noise like something clearing its throat high above us, and dark clouds spread rapidly across the sky. The air is filled with dampness and a strong grassy smell. I smooth my hair with my hand. Just as I thought. My hair, which has a slight wave, has gotten frizzy the way it always does before it rains. It's really frizzy, though—it must be about to pour. Tetsu and I quicken our pace, and head down the residential streets.

"Tomomi," Tetsu gasps, out of breath, "do you know why there are so many cats there?"

"Why?"

"People take their cats there to get rid of them. To throw them away. It's a cat dump. That's what the lady said. The park, too."

The sound of thunder is drawing closer, and we walk silently for a while through the darkness that thickens around us.

"I'm going to live there."

"In that junk heap?"

"Yeah."

"You just called it a cat dump!"

"It is. I'm going to sleep in that minibus. I'll be okay there."

"What do you mean you'll be okay?"

"I don't mean right now."

"That's crazy! Besides, it's impossible."

"But if—"

Just then a great rumbling noise like a giant opening a huge stone door sounds from the heavens.

What had Tetsu been about to say? *But if* . . . He is going to go live in that garbage dump if what happens? If he makes friends with the cats? If our father never comes home?

I think of suggesting that we run, but we are already completely out of breath. So we just keep on walking. Because I am staring straight ahead, I don't notice the man coming our way. By the time I do, all I can see are his eyes. They startle me, like a sudden flash of light in the darkness. It can have taken only two or three paces for us to pass each other. For an instant my mind goes blank. As he passes me, the man slips his hand under my sweater and squeezes my left breast.

I cannot even scream. I keep walking, as if hypnotized, and by the time I look back, no one is there.

"Tomomi, what is it?" Tetsu's face is questioning, his eyes blinking. He didn't notice. He didn't notice anything at all.

Suddenly it begins to pour so hard that we can't keep our eyes open. Soaked through, I keep on walking.

"Tomomi!" I turn. Tetsu looks like a drowned rat and his chin is trembling. I feel miserable.

The man was wearing gray coveralls. His hair, peppered with white, was curly, as if he had had it permed. His face was pale, his nose large, and his lips thin, with the lower one protruding slightly. It was hard to tell from his face whether he was old or young. And those eyes. Those eyes that gleamed so strangely. Why do I remember these details so clearly? I can still feel his fingers. They are digging into my flesh, twisting and turning, digging toward my heart, trying to rip it out.

I stand still in the rain and stare with horror at my body. My

67

flat chest is just starting to swell. It hurts when I run sometimes, but when I asked my mother to buy me a bra, she just laughed and said, "It's a little soon for that, don't you think?"

That man's gleaming eyes had known everything. That my mother scoffed at me, that I would be too chicken to scream, that Tetsu would not notice, or that even if he did, he was such a weakling that he couldn't do anything. He had seen through it all. Everything seems so pointless.

I pinch my left breast hard. As the pain numbs my body, I call on the monster within me for the first time in my life. "What's wrong with you? If you're going to awaken, isn't now the time? Show yourself and crush him beneath your feet! And these houses, my own house, the school, everything around me that pretends not to see—it's all a bunch of useless junk! Destroy it all!"

At that moment, thunder peals. The voice of the monster in my dreams is at long last approaching from the far ends of the sky. Or so it seems to me.

"Are you coming tomorrow morning? To see the cats and that lady?" Tetsu has climbed halfway up the ladder and pokes his head over the top of my bunk. I went straight to bed after taking a bath and eating dinner. Bed is the only place where I am safe.

There is a long red welt on Tetsu's cheek where I pinched him. I don't even remember why I did it. Probably it was because he picked at his food and asked stupid questions as usual. There is no other reason. There can't be. After all, what happened isn't his fault.

"You will come, won't you?"

I turn my back on him.

"Tomomi, what's wrong?" His voice, full of concern, sounds like an angel's. "Did something happen?"

He always does this. Even if I'm mean to him for no reason, ten minutes later he will be saying, "Tomomi, let's play." Or, "I'll share my cake with you." And that only irritates me more.

"Why don't you just go and live with her?" I say, with my back still toward him. "You're always talking about her. It drives me crazy."

"Don't you like her?"

"No, I don't."

"Why?" Tetsu sounds truly puzzled.

"I just don't, that's all." I feel like screaming. "Go on and feed those filthy cats with her," I snap. "You say you're looking for a dead cat and instead you end up feeding them. It's so stupid."

Tetsu climbs silently down the ladder and turns out the light. I have no idea what a terrible thing I have just said.

Seven

Everyone is chasing me. The guy with the smirk is in the lead. The gym teacher, Mr. Noguchi, is there, and so is Kumi, a girl who was in my class.

"I see it! There's the monster!"

"No, no. You've got it all wrong," I try to say, but my voice comes out in a strangled cry. I hate the sound. I was just trying to scare them, but now it has really become my voice. I try to explain. "You're wrong. I'm not a monster."

"Oh yeah? Then just what *are* you?" they all begin to clamor, jeering at me. "Yeah! What are you?"

I cannot answer. I think I am probably a girl, a junior-high-school student, or something like that, but I may not appear that way to them, because I'm not even sure of it myself . . .

My leg muscles have cramped; I can't move another step. I'm done for. My body turns mushy and begins to melt.

I stretch out my arms, reaching for help, and gasp at the sight of my hands. Those hands. The hairy, big-knuckled hands of that man. Everyone screams and scatters like baby spiders from a nest. I wave my hands violently, trying to shake them off like a pair of gloves. But the more I shake them, the larger they become.

I wake up but am unable to move for a moment. The air seems taut, and when I finally manage to twist my body toward the window, the sky is a leaden gray. I gaze fearfully at my hands and breathe a sigh of relief. They are my own hands, the nails, which I always chew, sunken into the thin flesh of the fingertips.

When I go downstairs, Grandpa calls out to me from the porch. "I made some noodles with egg."

"No thanks. I'm not hungry."

The wall clock says it is already past one. I stare vacantly at the pendulum for a while. So what happened yesterday wasn't a dream after all. Deep within my ears, thunder rumbles like some creature howling. Once again I look at my hands. The monster in my dreams has finally begun to reveal its shape. Surely because I summoned it . . .

"Hey!" Grandpa yells from the porch, and when I go to look he hands me the cord to the organ without even glancing at me. "Plug it in, will you?" He's removed the front panel, and the organ's dusty insides are showing.

"Come on. Hurry up."

I plug it in without a word and Grandpa flips the switch.

71

Unconsciously, I hold my breath and stare at the tips of Grandpa's fingers resting on the keys. *Three, two, one . . .*

There is no sound at all. It's not that I am expecting something beautiful, but there is nothing, not even the crackling static of last time. The organ sits like an anonymous bronze sculpture in a park, composed and silent.

Grandpa removes his fingers from the keys, fiddles with the volume, and tries out the foot pedals. I sigh and stand up to pull out the cord. "I knew it wouldn't work," I say.

Grandpa puffs out clouds of smoke and glares at the organ. Looking at him sitting on the porch wearing an old sweater with the elbows worn through, I feel even more lost.

"Why don't you just give up and come on inside? Even if you manage to fix it—"

"I wonder where Tetsu's got to?"

"Who cares?" He has probably gone back to the river, or Reed Marsh, or is staring stupidly at crushed cans at the recycling center.

"He didn't even come home for lunch. Would you go look for him?"

"What for? I'm not his keeper, am I?"

Grandpa just ignores the fact that I am mouthing off. I run upstairs. I don't want to go outside, no matter what.

I take the mirror out of my drawer and gaze into it, but it wavers in my hand, showing me only my plump upper lip, the little pimples forming around my nose, and my uneven bangs. The scissors won't do what I want, and my bangs, which were already too short, are now even shorter.

I crawl into bed, my head hurting for the first time in a few days. I hope it gets worse. I wish it would pound harder and harder until it splits like a strawberry run over by a car. Then maybe everyone would cry and say, "Poor Tomomi. She met such a horrible end."

But now it hurts so much that I can't even think anymore, and I close my eyes. I just want to go to sleep for a long, long time.

In my dreams, I can feel myself sleeping. I bob up and down on a stream of sleep, thinking, "More, more," and sinking deeper. I know someone came to wake me several times, but, as though bound hand and foot, I can't lift even a single finger.

When I finally do awake, however, it is so nice outside that I wonder what on earth I am doing sleeping in the middle of the day. I go downstairs and look at the calendar in the TV room. It is April 1. I slept right through the night without even eating supper. No wonder my legs feel so wobbly.

On the porch, Grandpa is removing the pedals from the organ. He shifts a wire cutter and a screwdriver alternately from one hand to the other, skillfully cutting the wires and undoing the screws. He carefully wipes each part he removes on a rag as though it were something precious and lays it out on the sunlit porch. The music stand, the pedals, even the backboard, riddled with holes, have been wiped clean of mold. The machine within is interconnected with different-colored wires.

"What are you doing? Taking it apart?"

"Mmm." Grandpa stretches his thickset back slightly. "Is your headache better?"

I sit down in a corner of the porch. I am feeling rather weak from having slept so long. "Where's Tetsu?" I ask.

"He's gone out." He takes off his glasses and peers at the wall clock in the shadowed room beyond. "I told him to come home for lunch this time."

The clock's hands show 9:30. Grandpa puts on his glasses again. He looks at me and says, "There's bread. Noodles for lunch okay?"

"Yeah."

"I can make some for you now if you don't want bread for breakfast."

"No, that's okay."

This is the first real spring day we've had. There is no wind, and the sunlight soaks slowly into my skin.

Grandpa turns the screwdriver in his hand, his face bright red with the effort. But it doesn't budge, and instead he strips the thread.

"What's the point in taking it apart, if you're just going to throw it away? I know where you can dump it—near the river. There's lots of junk there. A fridge, even a minibus."

Grandpa doesn't respond but continues to glare at the head of the screw. "Phew, this is a tough one," he says to himself, and his back hunches over even farther. He takes out the screws patiently, one by one, then cuts the wires that are sticking out all over the place to exactly the same length.

It is no use, no matter what I say. I just sit there staring blankly at what Grandpa is doing. But his movements are so precise and methodical that I find it hard to believe he is dismantling an organ. Squatting there, he looks more like an Inuit from the far north, skinning and dissecting his precious catch to share, wasting nothing, not its fur, its vital organs, or even its blood. I saw a TV program on Inuit hunters once. They did not appear savage or frightening, even though the screen was filled with crimson seal blood. The red meat laid carefully on the ice looked beautiful.

But it is not right to equate the organ with a seal. A seal is useful. Therefore it cannot be the same as a broken organ. Broken things, unnecessary things, useless things are discarded in the end. Because they are junk. And junk is just junk, nothing more.

Those cats who live in the broken bus, then, are they useless and unnecessary, too? Tetsu said people get rid of unwanted cats there. But cats are living creatures, not objects. It can't be right to throw cats away, no matter how ragged they are. It is not right. Then what about a broken organ?

But what Grandpa is doing still makes no sense to me.

In the end, Tetsu doesn't come back for lunch. He doesn't even come home when it gets dark and starts to rain. When Mom comes home, she tells me to go look for him.

"No," I say quietly.

"What is the matter with you?" my mother asks as she puts away the shopping bags.

"I don't want to go."

"And your hair. What did you do to it? It looks awful!"

I tug fiercely at my bangs.

"And the back is all scraggly."

"I don't care! It's fine like this."

"Tomorrow you will go straight to the hairdresser. And you haven't gone to Kikuya yet, either."

Kikuya is a clothing store run by an old lady who wears incredibly thick makeup. I was supposed to go there to pick up my junior-high-school uniform.

"It's *your* uniform. Be responsible for yourself!"

"I don't need a uniform."

"And just what do you intend to wear to school?"

"I'm not going to school."

My mother sighs. "Everyone is so selfish. You expect me to do everything." She turns the tap on forcefully and says, "Now hurry up! Go find Tetsu."

But, Mom, look how dark it is out there. And if I venture out alone, what if the same thing happens again? What if that man is there? I want to say it, but the words will not come. It wasn't my fault he did that to me, so why do I feel like it is?

"Well? Are you going or not?" My mother stops rinsing the rice and fixes her eyes on me as if this is my last chance.

"Why can't Grandpa go?"

"He's taking a bath. Are you going or not?"

"All right! I'm going!"

She turns her back on me as soon as she hears this, and runs the water violently again. She doesn't care about me at all. She couldn't care less what happens to me. It's always Tetsu, Tetsu, Tetsu.

"I'll go find Tetsu, Mom, if you go and find Dad."

The *swish-swish* of her hand in the water as she rinses the rice halts abruptly. But before she can turn around, I am out the door.

Huge drops of rain bounce off the gleaming black asphalt. I clutch the handle of my umbrella tightly and cross to the other side of the street whenever someone comes from the opposite direction. The black mouths of the shadow of a lamppost, a vacant lot, the dark doorway of an empty house open wide. I am so tense that by the time I reach the woman's apartment, all the strength seems to have been sapped from my knees.

Her window is pitch-black. She should be back from the park by now. I wonder what happened. The rain pelts down even harder, and as I huddle beneath my umbrella I suddenly hear my own words, "Why don't you just go and live with her?" That is what I had said. Surely Tetsu didn't think I was serious. The fluorescent bulb above the stairs flickers and then goes out.

But in my mind's eye I am looking at a night train setting off for a distant place. Tetsu and the woman sit facing each other, staring through the window at the city lights sparkling like stars. They look like mother and son.

Of course. Why shouldn't she want Tetsu for her son? Everyone who sees him says he's so cute they want to eat him. And Tetsu likes her a lot. Of course he doesn't want to come home. Our father isn't coming back, Mom is edgy, and then I go and say something mean to him like that. Would it still be kidnapping if Tetsu asked the lady to take him? What am I thinking? Still, she does live on her own, which must be lonely, and she is a bit strange, always feeding those stray cats and all.

Just then a huge black form appears. A long black arm reaches out and grabs my shoulders, which have stiffened in surprise. I scream.

"What are you so jumpy for? It's just me." A pair of eyes blink slowly against the rain that penetrates the depths of a rain hood. The woman.

"Oh! It's you," I exclaim. My blood, which had frozen for an instant, begins to circulate through my body again. The enormous black form was her bicycle covered with a black plastic garbage bag to keep it dry.

"What's up? What're you doing here?"

"I thought Tetsu might be with you." My face is burning.

The woman shakes her head. "I haven't seen him since I saw you both the other day."

I was sure that he had been with her yesterday and today. So where was he?

"Is he missing?" She pulls her rain hood off beneath the shelter of the apartment eaves. She has dark smudges beneath her eyes as if she has rubbed them with soot.

"You're soaking wet!" I fold up my umbrella and peer at her face.

"I'm all right."

"The cats?"

"Yes."

"You could at least take a day off when it rains."

"Even if it rains, you still get hungry, right?" But her voice seems listless. "Do you want to come in? I have some ice cream."

She holds on to the iron railing on the stairs and laughs a little. How could I have suspected her, even for a moment, of kidnapping Tetsu?

"No thanks. Tetsu might be home by now." I unfurl my umbrella and dash off through the rain. Maybe I look as if I'm running away but I tear down the dark road anyway, heedless of the puddles.

That night, the monster shows its shape a little more, a black shadow engulfing the asphalt glittering in the sunlight. At first I don't think it's me. But the fuzzy hair moves at the same time as I do.

Eight

The next-door neighbor is shouting. "What can he be bellowing about?" I wonder absently, coming awake. His voice sounds very close. "Well, it wasn't my son!" I hear my mother say, shrilly. I sit up abruptly. He is at the front door.

"Why don't I ask him myself!" The old man raises his voice.

I glance down into the bunk below me. Tetsu's eyes are wide open and he lies on his back, humming to himself. But I can see that he is as stiff as an Egyptian mummy under his quilt.

"Tetsu," I say, and he stops humming. He is staring straight up. That means he is staring at the bottom of my bunk, which has regularly spaced small holes bored through it. He often counts them. Sometimes he counts five hundred, sometimes five thousand. Recently he told me that he had counted three thousand two hundred and fifty-six. But today he seems to be staring through and beyond the board itself, higher and higher, and it makes me uneasy.

"Tetsu, last night—you didn't . . ." I begin, but he starts humming again.

By the time I got back last night, Tetsu was already home. No matter how many times I asked him where he had been, he refused to answer. During supper, he didn't complain about his food the way he usually does, but sat silently shoveling it into his mouth, forcing it down while he glared at the scratches in the tabletop. My mother filled our rice bowls in silence and ate without saying a word. Probably because I told her she should go find Dad. But I didn't feel like apologizing, so I ate silently, pushing the rice like a lump of stone down my throat.

"This pickle is a bit salty," Grandpa remarked.

"It's the kind I always buy," my mother replied.

"But it tastes different. Did you try it?"

"Then I won't buy it anymore," she said without tasting it.

That was the only conversation during the entire meal, and then we all retreated silently to our rooms. Now that I think of it, Tetsu even brushed his teeth without being told.

I dress hurriedly and rush downstairs. For a moment I almost stop breathing. There is a dustpan at the old man's feet. And sprawled across it is a cat. A single glance is enough to see that it is dead.

"Bring your boy here. If you don't, then I'll go get him myself!" He is shaking his foot, thin as a bird's, to remove his sandal. My mother reaches out as if to say, "Now wait a minute," but the old man grabs her wrist with surprising swiftness. His hand is covered in liver spots and gnarled blue veins.

"Ow!"

The old man won't let go. "Call your brother." The sight of the old man's face, deep purple with rage, is seared upon my brain.

"Don't bother, Tomomi," my mother says frantically, wrenching her arm from his grasp.

In contrast, the old man says coolly, "Well, now. Look at that." Tetsu's sneaker is lying in the front entrance where he kicked it off the night before. It is covered in mud.

"He left his footprints in the backyard. They're there, clear as day, all the way from the wall."

I sink to my knees. This must be a bad dream. *Wake up. Wake up.*

"Come and see for yourself. Let's clear this up right now."

My mother is standing ramrod-straight, refusing to be a party to this. "Don't talk such nonsense."

The old man looks surprised for a moment. "That's it, Mom, don't back down," I think. But then he says, "I want to talk to the boy's father," and suddenly my mother looks frightened.

"His father, I say," the old man demands. My mother's sudden deflation has not escaped his notice. "It's no use talking about it without his father."

Mom, why? Why let a little thing like that get to you? Don't let him do this to you. He's not playing fair.

Just then Grandpa appears. The next-door neighbor begins to speak, but with great dignity Grandpa kneels on the hall floor, bends forward, his back like a large mountain, and bows his head. It is not only his weight that makes him appear imposing, and my mother, the next-door neighbor, and I all fall silent for a moment. Without raising his head, Grandpa says quietly, "I will question my grandson very carefully. Please be so kind as to leave it at that for today." Then, raising his head slowly, he adds, "And of course, you may leave the cat here." He looks up at the other man calmly.

The next-door neighbor grabs his dustpan, dumping the cat, and stomps off muttering, "Darn right I will!"

The cat, pelted by last night's rain, is drenched. Its dark striped fur is falling off in patches and it is filthy. It must have been a stray.

"It looks as if it died of some illness. I'll get rid of it," Grandpa says, standing up slowly. His previous dignity has disappeared. "Don't touch it."

My mother is staring off into the darkness of the kitchen. Turning around, I see Tetsu standing there, still wearing his pajamas. His face is pale.

"Tetsu?"

But he doesn't seem to hear me. He is looking straight at the cat. His bare feet make a sucking sound as he steps onto the cold concrete and stands silently beside it. Then he crouches down and hugs the wretched corpse with its fur falling out tightly to him. Not one of us tries to stop him. He is crying. With his cheek pressed against the stiffened, ragged corpse, he opens and closes his mouth, gasping for air like someone who wants to scream but has lost his voice. He cries and cries.

We go to Reed Marsh and bury the cat.

"Is this where you found it?"

"Mmm." Tetsu carefully lays some loose moss on top of the damp earth of the burial mound.

I mimic him, gently caressing the soft moss. This must be what it feels like to pet a cat, I think to myself. Then I say, "I'm sorry," in a small voice.

Tetsu shakes his head, drawing his hand away from the moss. "I lied to Grandpa. I told him I didn't do it." He wraps his arms around his knees, still squatting on his haunches. His eyes look like cloudy mirrors, reflecting the green of the moss and ferns, the marsh water, the leaden sky. I wonder if Grandpa knew he was lying.

The wooden box that we buried the cat in was an old one that Grandpa dug out of the storage room. "Here. Put the poor thing in this," he said, when Tetsu showed no sign of releasing the dead cat even though he had stopped crying. "This is the box from those sweet citron buns you used to love when you were little," he added. Tetsu gazed blankly at it for a while, and then, rubbing his eyes, announced, "I remember this box."

"I can't tell Grandpa. There's no way I could," Tetsu says. Then, muttering, "I hate lying. I just hate it," he picks up his shovel and stands up.

I can hear footsteps on the ceiling. Heavy footsteps. *Thump, thump.* It must be that big black cat which left a minute ago.

All the cats are outside napping in the sun because we have taken over the minibus at the junk heap.

We never actually decided to do this. It's just that no other place came to mind. Neither of us wanted to go home, and Tetsu kept stumbling and seemed too tired to spend the day walking around. I don't think he slept much last night.

He is lying down on the backseat humming to himself and jiggling his legs. I sit on one of the double seats with my back leaning against the window, biting my nails. When I get tired of biting my nails I pull out strands of hair from my head. The next-door neighbor is probably out in his garden as usual, over-trimming the trees or spraying pesticide. If he's thinking of Tetsu at all, he's probably just thinking that he is weird.

"Tetsu."

"Mmm."

"Listen. We're not going home and we won't go to school either when the new term starts. We'll just stay here—at night, too—like camping."

I don't know what's made me say this, but once I've said it, it seems like a great idea.

Tetsu sits up and looks at me a little strangely, then blinks slowly. "Okay."

In the early afternoon we go to the shopping center. We buy croquettes at the meat shop and sit on a bench in a nearby park. It is the same park where the woman feeds the cats. Not having eaten since breakfast, we gobble down the croquettes without even bothering to put sauce on them.

"I wonder if we could make some money by taking the empty cans and scraps of metal to the place where that lady works," I suggest. "We could carry small things at least."

"Yeah, maybe," Tetsu says, but his voice sounds feeble.

"Come on, cheer up."

"Mmm." He nods without looking up and finally swallows the last mouthful, which he has been chewing for ages.

"Where do you think the cats are?" I look around. "They never come out except when it's time to be fed."

"Mmm."

"There're too many dogs and kids around."

"Mmm."

"I wonder where they're hiding."

"I don't know." He sounds irritated. I guess just the thought of meeting a cat is painful to him. That must be why he stayed in the bus and would not even look out the window at them. I brush the croquette crumbs off his pants. He sits silently, without resisting.

"Let's go."

"Mmm." But he is reluctant to move.

I turn back to him, exasperated, wondering what to do, when a cat suddenly appears from a clump of weeds behind the bench. It is white with round black spots, like a lump of pounded sweet rice with black beans stuck in it. It presses its face close to Tetsu's knees, then sniffs the tips of my fingers and licks them a little with its raspy tongue. Shocked, I whip my hand away. Tetsu stares at the cat, then exclaims, "Oh! I know! It smells the croquettes."

"We've never seen this cat before, have we?"

Tetsu looks around stealthily.

"What?"

"Shh!"

I hear thin, shrill voices crying, "*Mii, mii, mii.*" I look around, too, and see the white face of a single kitten with big ears sticking out of a cardboard box.

"Is this your baby?" I ask. The cat stays sitting at Tetsu's feet, looking at me and blinking its eyes, which are encrusted with discharge.

"*Mii, mii, mii.*" The sound grows and fades, several voices intertwining like fine threads threatening to become tangled.

Tetsu stands and steps onto the grass. The plaintive crying stops, and this time three kittens pop their heads over the edge of the box. They stare at us, the space between their eyes so wide they look like frogs.

Tetsu looks at me, blinks hard several times, and then carefully takes another step. The kittens hiss. Despite their tiny size, they are trying their best to bare their fangs.

"They're angry," Tetsu says, looking at me and pointing toward the kittens.

"They have very bad manners. Why don't you catch them?"

"No, remember what the lady said?" He looks at me accusingly. "Don't try anything stupid, Tomomi."

"What do you mean? What are you looking at me like that for?" Even the mother cat is looking at me suspiciously.

"Tomomi, let's go get our stuff. And we can get some milk for them, too."

"Stuff? What stuff?"

"Do you have amnesia, Tomomi? What about your idea of sleeping in the bus?" he snaps. His former despondency seems to have completely vanished.

An alarm clock, a flashlight, an illustrated book on animals, a sweater, comic books, a mirror and hairbrush, scissors, my piggy bank, the bankbook and bank card for my savings account where I keep the money I get at New Year's, five packages of instant chicken noodles, a package of cookies, four oranges, and a bag of Grandpa's cough drops. This is enough to fill our knapsacks full to bursting.

"Can I take just one more book? It's about trains and airplanes and stuff."

"No. If we don't hurry up, Grandpa will catch us."

"But I want to take it."

He won't give up, so I unpack my comic books to make room. We put on our knapsacks and go downstairs. I start putting on my shoes at the back door when Tetsu pokes me.

"What?"

"We forgot the milk."

"Oh, right."

I go back to the kitchen and notice that I left the closet door wide open when I was looking for the noodles. I close it quietly and take out a half-empty carton of milk from the fridge and a saucer that is lying on the counter, and return to the back door.

"Here. Take this. I'll lock the door."

I lock it carefully so as not to make any noise. We tiptoe beneath the window of the storage room, where Grandpa is, and begin running as soon as we reach the road.

With our packs on our backs, we head straight for the park. When we look inside the cardboard box on the grass, the mother cat blinks her eyes and gives a short mew, then climbs out. Tetsu and I squat down and pour the milk we have brought into the saucer and watch her pink tongue flicking in and out as she drinks.

"You want to pet her?"

"You try it, Tomomi."

"No, you do it, Tetsu."

His hand, taut with tension, is rigid straight down to the tips of his fingers. Shaking, he stretches it toward the cat, but just before he touches her back, she looks at him. She mews again.

"I changed my mind," Tetsu says, hiding both hands between his legs as he squats. "I won't bother you. Go ahead. Drink some more."

The sound of the cat's tongue slurping milk resumes.

"Remember when she licked my finger before? Her tongue was rough and raspy."

"I know that. I read in a book that cats have rough tongues. Do you know why?"

"No."

"To groom their fur when they lick themselves. It's like a comb."

"Really?"

"That's why they swallow their fur. And they eat grass so they can cough up the fur that's in their stomachs."

"You sure know a lot," I say, impressed. He squirms with embarrassment and then asks in a small voice, "What did it feel like?"

"Raspy. It kind of tickled."

"Hmm."

I put a drop of milk on my fingertip and wipe it on the palm of his hand. "Excuse me a minute," I say to the cat, removing the saucer and putting Tetsu's hand under her nose instead. She pulls back at first but then stretches out her head again and swiftly licks the drop of milk.

"Tomomi! It really *is* raspy!" Tetsu exclaims, his nostrils quivering.

"Told you," I say, giving the saucer back to the cat.

Having finished the milk, she returns to the box and begins to nurse her kittens. We peer stealthily inside and can see them snuggled against their mother's tummy, their whole bodies convulsing with each gulp. *Glug, glug.*

"They've been thrown away. For sure," Tetsu whispers, as though he's afraid they might hear.

The cardboard box is swollen with last night's rain. To be thrown away when you have just had kittens . . . How horrible, I think, but the mother cat seems very contented nursing, her eyes half-closed. She looks as if she's about to fall asleep.

Tetsu is falling asleep, too. His hands, which are wrapped around his knees as he crouches, loosen and drop to the ground, and he sits down with a thud, then rubs his eyes.

"Don't rub your eyes."

"I'm sleepy." He has rubbed them so much that the lids have extra wrinkles and they are stuck wide open.

90

"Why don't you go home and have a nap?"

"Go home?" Tetsu looks at me in surprise.

"You know where I mean," I say, and grabbing both of our knapsacks, I stand up.

There is a blazing orange sunset and the slightly sour smell of cats. The inside of the bus is full of the warmth stored up during the day. Tetsu is sound asleep. The black cat that was here earlier and a cat with patches the color of milky coffee on its back come in through the half-open door and start licking themselves. Although they won't sit on the same seat with us, they appear to be getting used to us.

I sit in the driver's seat and watch the sun sinking behind the expressway in front of us. It seems to be looking right back at me. I grasp the steering wheel. Someday even the sun will become like this pile of junk, no longer useful. Just as people, no matter how fulfilled or worthy they may be, must die, so, too, the sun will someday burn itself out. I wonder if the sun knows that. And if it does know, how can it burn so brightly?

From behind me, I hear the sound of dragging footsteps approaching, feet half slipped into sneakers. It's Tetsu.

"You woke up."

Tetsu's forehead, covered in a greasy film from sleeping, is dyed crimson. "It's too bright," he says, yawning enormously. "You know when the sun goes down and disappears behind the horizon? Right at that second there's a flash of green light."

"You've seen it?"

"No. I read it in a book." He sits down on the single passenger seat closest to the front, takes off his sneakers, and pulls his knees up to his chest. "It said that you can see it only where there are no buildings or anything in the way."

We sit motionless, watching the setting sun until it vanishes from the square of sky framed by the expressway and the buildings on the other side. Everything around us gradually darkens to gray. We are like two nomads on horseback watching the green flash at the horizon beyond a never-ending grassy plain.

Nine

"That lady's late." Tetsu has been silent so long that his voice is hoarse. It's the time of day when it is neither dark nor light, when the only color that is really visible is white, which sticks out as if coated with fluorescent paint. Tetsu's face looks like the white kernel of an acorn with the hard shell peeled away.

"We could walk out and meet her, if you want."

"No. Let's wait. She'll be really surprised to see us here."

The cats are hungry and they look at our faces, waving their tails and crying. It seems we have no choice, so I take out the instant noodles, crumbling them into little pieces, and try feeding them. Some of them sniff it and look at me, rather puzzled. Others turn their backs haughtily. But in the end all five packages are gone. They shake their heads back and forth as they chew, as though having trouble eating, but I can hear a crunching noise from their mouths.

"I wonder if she took the day off." Tetsu is crouching down, and he rubs his chin against his knees.

"Well, wherever she is, there's not much we can do about it. Maybe we should eat, too."

Three cookies each. We chew the slightly soggy cookies slowly, washing them down with mouthfuls of milk from the carton we brought for the cats this afternoon.

"Good, isn't it?"

"Mmm."

Tetsu giggles. We share an orange, licking the juice that falls on our hands.

"Here, Tomomi," Tetsu says, passing me a stick of chewing gum. "It's a substitute for brushing your teeth." But then he suddenly falls silent, staring at the gum he is holding out. It must remind him of home. Because he talked about brushing teeth. And he's probably thinking about the dead cat, too. I take the wrapper off the gum and poke it against his lips.

"Know what?" I say. "Chewing gum makes you smart."

"Really?"

We chew the gum vigorously, with loud smacking noises.

That night a huge moon rises. It is barely past full, and looks like a pancake just poured into the pan and waiting to be cooked. Cat eyes gleam in the darkness, and Tetsu hops about on top of the junk heap.

At first I think my watch is broken, because the hands point to eight o'clock even though I feel sure that it's the middle of the night. I take out the alarm clock from my knapsack. It says the same thing. Eight o'clock. No wonder I'm not sleepy. Time must be like socks and chewing gum. It can shrink and stretch.

Turning on the flashlight, I decide to count the money in my piggy bank. Four five-hundred-yen pieces, eight one-hundred-yen pieces, enough ten-yen pieces to fill the palm of one hand, and a bunch of five- and one-yen coins. With this much money, we could buy thirty croquettes. I have started counting the ten-yen pieces and have just reached twenty when I hear a foot tread on the step at the bus door. I lift my face at the quiet, heavy sound. It is my mother.

"What are you doing here?" she asks in a sharp voice.

I don't know what to do, so I keep counting the ten-yen pieces. 28, 29, 30 . . . It's not as though I didn't expect this. But I am all confused inside, so I no longer know what's what.

"How did you know we were here?" I mumble without looking up.

"I went looking for you, and Mr. Taguchi told me that he saw you in the garbage dump when he was out for a walk."

"This . . ." I start to say, but stop.

"What?" Her voice is very quiet. Too quiet.

"This isn't a garbage dump. You aren't supposed to throw garbage here."

I point to a sign, almost completely buried, that says NO DUMPING, as though looking for support. Tetsu is standing precariously on top of a toaster watching us. My mother sighs. A long, long sigh.

"Look. You're not a child anymore. You're already in junior high school."

I wish she wouldn't say it like that. After all, it's not as if I'm going into junior high because I want to.

"Tomomi."

"Yes?"

"Let's go home."

"Mom, please . . ." I can't finish. My mother looks at me steadily. "I want to stay here tonight."

All expression drains from my mother's face, as though her face itself is melting in water. But only for a single instant. The next moment she says, "So, you hate our house that much? Fine, then, do as you please." And she gets off the bus. Tetsu looks at her, then looks at me standing in the doorway, then back at her again. She climbs quickly up the embankment and disappears down the other side without using the path along the top.

"Tomomi. Are you going home?" He walks over and looks up at me where I stand on the step.

I shake my head and place the knapsack carefully back on the seat. My mother's words, *You're not a child anymore*, resound loudly in my mind.

"If you want to go home, Tetsu, go ahead."

"What about you?"

"I'm staying here."

I cannot go home. I feel sorry for my mother, but if I go home now, I will only be miserable. I may not be a child, but I am not yet as much of an adult as my mother would like me to be.

". . ."

"Cat."

"Tree."

"Elephant."

"Train."

We are playing a word game. Each word we say has to start with the last letter in the word said before it. Back and forth.

"Nap."

"Pilaf."

"Fart." Tetsu makes a rude noise and bursts out laughing.

"Trailer."

"Rainbow."

"Wee-wee." Tetsu bursts out laughing again, overcome with glee.

"Knock it off, Tetsu!"

" 'Wee-wee' ends with 'e,' not 'k.' Can't you spell?"

" 'E'? All right, then. Enough!" I shine the flashlight on my watch. "It's already ten o'clock. It's way past your bedtime."

"It's okay."

Tetsu is so wound up that I almost think there is something wrong with him. Maybe it is because Mom came.

"Come on. Just a little more."

"Oh, all right. Where were we?"

" 'E,' it was 'e.' "

"Eagle."

"Engine!" Tetsu answers promptly.

"Eagle!"

"Engine!"

We continue rhythmically chanting, "Eagle!" "Engine!" "Eagle!" "Engine!"

Tetsu is so excited he screeches. He is acting like a five-year-old.

"Enough. Now go to sleep. We're getting up early tomorrow," I insist. I take out a sweater and tuck it around his shoulders and neck while, eyes sparkling, he goes on chanting "Eagle, engine," over and over, like some kind of tongue twister.

"I'm going to sleep," I announce firmly. I leave Tetsu on the backseat and lie down on the seat in front of him with my knees drawn up and my arms wrapped around them.

"Tomomi?"

I breathe deeply, pretending to be asleep. I can feel him looking over the seat at me. Then I hear a small sigh of resignation.

I wonder what my mother did after she left. Is she in bed by now? When Tetsu falls asleep, maybe I should go and take a look at the house just to see. But if I do that, I will have to take the pitch-black path along the river . . . Curled up on the rough seat of the bus, shrinking with cold, I start to wonder what on earth I am doing here at this hour of the night. Maybe this was a mistake after all.

"Tetsu?"

There is no answer. Has he gone to sleep already? I whisper to myself, "Eagle, engine, eagle, engine, eagle, engine . . ."

I sit up and press my forehead against the windowpane, looking up at the sky. The moon is hidden and everything around us seems sunk in deep, dark water. I can hear the sound of Tetsu breathing. And the noise of the cars on the expressway. But that is not all.

There is a low moaning. I freeze and listen carefully. The sound grows gradually louder and the number of voices increases until suddenly the air is rent by a loud screech. What could it be? The bus is surrounded by eerie moans and screeches. It is as if something is calling me from the darkness.

"Tetsu." I reach out a hand and shake him. "Mmm," he mumbles in reply, but he is still firmly wrapped in sleep.

Just then the door of the bus creaks.

Someone is there.

A huge dark shadow enters stealthily. Stooping under the low ceiling, it comes slowly toward the backseats, toward us.

Thump . . . thump . . . thump . . .

I feel as though the tongue of some cold, bloodless creature has licked my back and I cannot breathe.

The man from the other day . . .

It must be him. He must have been following us since then. What should I do? I can't get away, and there is no one to rescue me.

Facing me, he leans forward.

"Eeeeyaaaah!" I raise the flashlight high and at the same moment a voice says, "Tomomi?"

"Grandpa?" I gasp, but it's too late. In that instant of revelation the flashlight connects. He grabs the top of his head and slumps into the seat.

"Grandpa! Are you all right?" I hastily turn on the flashlight and he screws his face up against the bright glare.

"What? Grandpa?" Tetsu remarks groggily.

"There's no blood . . ."

"I'm all right," Grandpa says, and he pushes my arm holding the flashlight with which I have been investigating the damage as if to say, "Enough already." Grandpa hates people making a fuss over him. He twists his stout frame around on the seat and looks outside, fascinated. "What an amazing place!"

"That square hump over there, that's a fridge. And that thing there, that's a toilet seat. Tomomi stepped on it the other day." Tetsu is chattering and rubbing his eyes when the moaning starts up again.

"Shhh!"

"Tomomi, what's that?"

With sudden ear-piercing wails, two shadows tumble across the scraps of sheet metal and vanish. Cats. Tetsu opens the window and leans out, yelling, "Hey, you! No fighting!" There is silence for one second and then the high-pitched voices take up their eerie melody again.

"Maybe they're turning into goblin cats," Tetsu muses. He pulls himself back inside and starts rocking back and forth as if he can't decide whether to go outside and check or not.

"Grandpa?"

"Mmm," he grunts, but his eyes are still fixed on the darkness outside. "Tomomi, isn't that TV over there still pretty new?"

"I didn't throw it away, so how am I supposed to know," I think. It is certainly newer than Grandpa's old wreck, though.

"Grandpa, did Mom tell you to come?"

He turns to look at me. "No," he says. "Your mom's okay."

"I wasn't worried about her. I just wondered why you came, that's all."

Grandpa stands up, leans over the seat in front, and with a grunt pulls up a big paper shopping bag. A fluffy blanket appears from inside it.

"I thought you were going to tell us to go home."

He folds the shopping bag meticulously, making crisp creases at the folds.

"Mmm. It's been aired in the sun today," Tetsu exclaims in a muffled voice, his face buried in the blanket.

"That weird yowling noise the cats make, they're looking for a mate. They don't do it all year round. The season should be almost over," Grandpa explains. "Just leave them alone. It's their way of dating," he adds to Tetsu, who is so distracted by the noise that he can't sit still.

With Grandpa in the middle, the three of us huddle under the blanket and talk in whispers, enveloped by the smell of sun-aired blanket and cigarette smoke from Grandpa's clothes. Chubby old Grandpa is nice and warm.

All the cats in the bus are sleeping peacefully, ignoring the noisy dating going on outside. Some are curled up on their own, while others, like us, are all in a furry lump. When our voices get too loud, Tetsu and I both whisper, "Shhh."

"Shhh, shhhh, shhhh."

I hear the peaceful sound of deep breathing. It's Tetsu. A minute ago he was giggling and fooling around, and now he's sound asleep.

"You want a cough drop?" I ask Grandpa just for the sake of saying something.

"Mmm. I might at that."

I take the bag out of my knapsack and put two cough drops on my hand, then snuggle back under the blanket. They are Grandpa's. I snitched them from the kitchen and of course he is probably well aware of that, but still he looks pleased as he pops one into his mouth. We roll them around slowly on our tongues.

"So, shall we go to sleep?"

"Mmm," I say, although I don't want to go to sleep at all.

"Good night, then."

Ten

A crow caws even though it is the middle of the night. Just one . . . I close my eyes and follow the sound as it recedes, and the sound of the cars on the expressway becomes a band of light that begins to flow. My body floats up and flies as if it is sliding along that band.

I am dreaming. But by the time I realize it, I am high, high up in the sky and return seems impossible. Flying along the narrow intersecting roads, I see a familiar tall concrete building among the houses below. The school. I see the faces of my teacher and classmates lined up at the window of our classroom.

"Look, everybody! I'm flying through the sky." But no one waves to me. They are not even smiling. A gust of wind blows past, then stops.

Everything spread out below me stands silent and still within a gray light. The endless roofs are black and cold, like the surface of the sea, hundreds of fathoms deep. The silence covers everything, even the classroom windows. Why can I see everyone's faces so clearly when they are so far away? None of them have eyes. Two empty black holes stare out at me from each face.

They are all dead.

"Tomomi?"

Someone grabs my arm and I shake myself free. I awake with a start to find myself chilled to the bone.

"What's up?" Grandpa's voice sounds just the same. Maybe he wasn't asleep. I let out a small breath and the smell of the blanket comes back to me, enveloping me.

"Grandpa? Do you ever dream?"

"Sure I do."

"What about?"

"Grandma," he answers after a slight pause. "Oh, so she's alive after all, I think. And then I wake up." His eyes are closed and he seems far away from me. I wish he would do something to bring himself back. Even smoke a cigarette.

"Grandma? What's she like?"

"Just like always."

"Like always? What's that like?"

"Hmmm."

"I only remember the way she was in the hospital. When she kept groaning in pain." Grandpa turns and reaches out his arm to get a better look at my face, but I push his hand away. "And I wonder if I will die like that."

"Do you have nightmares about Grandma?" he says in surprise.

"No, that's not what I mean," I say hastily, and Grandpa mumbles that he just wondered because I was moaning in my sleep.

"I dream about monsters. That I turn into a monster."

We are both silent for a moment. He pats the back of my hand and says, "So Tomomi is a monster?"

"Yes."

"A bad one?"

"I'm serious!" I say sharply, and Grandpa's hand freezes. He pulls it away. "It's true," I add weakly, as though trying to excuse myself. But I can't explain any further. I just can't put it into words.

I thought he had gone to sleep, but suddenly Grandpa begins to talk. "I must have been about your age. My uncle lived in Shanghai."

"Shanghai? You mean China?"

"Yup."

"Your uncle? Is he still alive?"

"No, he's dead now. But he bought me some running shoes in Shanghai and sent them to me. They were very fashionable and the toes were trimmed in dark red rubber. They fit snug and the soles were sturdy. I almost flew when I ran. Everyone

105

envied me. Some kids couldn't even afford regular running shoes in those days."

What is he going on about, I wonder. His slightly raspy voice swells and fades in the night air.

"One day those shoes were gone from the shoe cupboard at school."

"They were stolen?"

"Yes. And I had a pretty good idea who did it. He was the poorest kid in our class and he often stared at my shoes. Once he had asked me to let him try them on, but I refused. Even though I had let other kids who asked, I didn't want to let him."

"Why not?"

I feel his body move slightly and know that he is nodding to himself. "Because I didn't like him. His jacket was in rags and during lunchtime, when everyone ate their lunches that they brought from home, he always disappeared."

"Maybe he didn't have any food to bring. Didn't you feel sorry for him?"

"I should have felt sorry for him. But his eyes always had a hard gleam in them and he never talked to anyone unless he had to. Everyone said he was arrogant. Everyone hated him. Everyone."

"And did he really steal your shoes?" I raise my voice intentionally and Grandpa purses his lips, mouthing *Shhh*.

"I didn't know for sure. But I told all my friends that he did."

"Even though there was no proof?"

"Yes. I was sure it was him. When I was telling everyone

that they were gone, I looked at his face and knew that he did it. And because nobody liked him anyway, everyone believed me when I accused him. He stopped coming to school."

The cats outside have suddenly become very quiet. I can feel Grandpa's heart beating: *thump, thump.*

"My teacher called me over. The boy's name was Takashi. He told me to go to Takashi's house and ask him to come back to school. He said that it was my fault Takashi didn't come to school anymore. I was already feeling a little guilty, so when the teacher blamed it on me and made it look like I was the bad guy, it made me even angrier. It really got me that the teacher would take the side of such a dim-witted, shabby-looking kid. But still I went. That same day, after school, I went to his house. Because I believed that the teacher must be right.

"It was awful, that house. It was standing all alone by the river. It wasn't even fit to be called a house. It was just a bunch of boards and rags tacked together and held down with stones so it wouldn't blow away in the wind. I ducked my head under a straw mat hanging over the doorway and asked for Takashi. A woman—his mother, I guessed—was lying down inside with some small listless children. Now that I think of it, she was probably sick. Anyway, she tried to get up, but Takashi, as if protecting her, stood up and glared at me. I just stood there, stunned, and he practically pushed me outside, saying, 'Whadya want?' He had a strange accent, and it occurred to me that that might be the reason he didn't talk much. It was the first time I had thought of that."

Grandpa stops talking and coughs deep in his throat, trying not to wake Tetsu.

"You want another cough drop?"

"No, thanks."

"Did you apologize to him?"

"Yes," he says and suddenly coughs loudly. Tetsu groans and rolls over. Carefully covering him up again, Grandpa continues. "I apologized. I told him to come back to school. That the teacher was waiting. He just stared at me. I thought that it would work out, but it didn't. He said, 'If you're going to apologize, do it right. Get down on your knees.' 'You little creep!' I thought to myself. But my teacher's face floated into my mind and I did as he said. I got down on my knees on the gravel along the riverbed and bowed my head to the ground, saying, 'I'm really sorry.' 'Say it louder,' he said, and I looked up into his face. His eyes were like the pointed end of a freshly oiled chisel. It didn't seem wise to disobey.

"Just then his little sister came out from behind the straw mat of that dirty old hut. She must have been about five years old, but she was horribly thin. Her face and body were so skinny she didn't look human. But her eyes were round and she looked at me as I knelt on the ground, and smiled and said, 'Are you Takashi's friend?' I thought she looked cute, but there was something strange about Takashi, the way he looked at her. Then I saw. She was wearing great floppy running shoes! With dark red rubber trim."

"Your running shoes?"

"Yes." He sighs. "Do you mind if I smoke?"

"Go ahead," I say. It is the first time anyone has ever asked me that, and I am startled.

He leans forward a little, pulls his arms out from under the blanket, takes a cigarette from his shirt pocket under his sweater, and lights it. He takes so long inhaling that it makes me squirm. He stopped talking right in the middle of the story. The tip of the cigarette glows brighter, shedding light on his square fingers, and smoke fans out. There is a rustling sound and a cat near the front goes out the door. I guess cats don't like cigarette smoke.

"So what happened?" I prompt him, unable to stand it any longer. He stubs out the cigarette carefully in the ashtray attached to the back of the seat, throws the butt away, and puts both arms back under the blanket.

"At first the only thing I could think of was the running shoes. That's why I jumped on the little girl and tried to take them off. But, of course, she struggled. I could hardly believe such a thin little thing could roll herself up so stubbornly, like a turtle. And when I tried to pull them off by force, she kicked wildly. I was so furious I hit her. Over and over. Takashi jumped on my back, yelling, 'Stop! Stop!' I was livid. 'Damn it all! You're the thief! You made me grovel when you're a dirty liar!' That's what I thought. But . . ." He nods again, as if trying to encourage himself to go on.

"But it was his little sister that I took it out on. Even though it was Takashi who had done wrong, I never even looked at him, but hit his sister instead. You know why?"

"Because she was wearing your running shoes?"

109

"No," he replied. "I knew why. I knew that if I wanted to hurt Takashi, the best way was to hurt his sister. That's why I hit her. And I didn't just hit her. I screamed at her, 'Your brother's a thief!' over and over again. Takashi pleaded with me to stop, and gradually I could hear tears in his voice. Then suddenly his sister stopped struggling and said, 'Takashi, is it really true?' That was the first and last time I ever saw him cry, because he never came to school again.

"I have never felt so bad in all my life. To beat up his poor little sister who didn't do anything. If I was going to hit someone, it would have been better to hit Takashi. I never imagined that I could act so mean just because of a pair of running shoes." He falls silent again.

"And the running shoes?"

"I never wore them." His body seems to shrink as if all the air has been knocked out of him. "I got them back, but I couldn't bear to wear them. I left them in the very back of the shoe cupboard, and then one day I threw them in the river."

I can hear the sound of the running shoes hitting the water. Grandpa was a monster when he hit that little girl. He was possessed by a monster, body and soul.

"But I decided then and there that I would never do something like that again. It's better to have nothing at all than to fight over material things, and that is the code by which I have lived my life ever since."

He moves his shoulders slightly as if to ask me whether I understand. I am unable to reply; my body is rigid. I know too well that that's the kind of person Grandpa is. If he had never met the monster within him, would he be a different person? Does he believe it was a good thing to meet that monster?

"What should you do when you've done something you regret, and there's no going back?" I ask in a hoarse voice.

Grandpa sits motionless, waiting for me to continue.

"When Grandma was in the hospital, I wished the awful noise of those machines would stop. I thought that she would be better off dead." I think I am going to cry. But my chest just feels tight. Not a single teardrop comes. I have not cried for a long time.

"It's true. Grandma was miserable in the hospital," Grandpa says quietly. "You didn't do anything bad, Tomomi. Grandma knows that, too."

But it has got nothing to do with whether she was miserable or not. At the time, I had felt numb, as if my heart was anesthetized. The only feeling I can think of that it resembled is that of surprise. Like when you are so surprised you cannot even speak. Then suddenly I had heard a voice within me saying, "She'd be better off dead."

"Tomomi."

"Huh?" Grandpa's voice startles me.

"If you'd been younger, you wouldn't have been able to feel Grandma's pain like that. To understand that sometimes it is better to die than to suffer."

That's true, I think. And when he says it, the feeling inside my chest suddenly eases.

A light shines, wavering as though I am looking at it through water. The clouds race away at high speed, a golden curtain opening, and the moon is revealed like a queen.

111

"Look how high it's climbed."

"Shall we go outside and look, Tomomi?"

"Mmm."

Grandpa spreads the blanket over Tetsu and heads toward the door.

"Tetsu, the moon is gorgeous. Do you want to see?"

"No, thanks. I'll eat later," he replies clearly, and even though I shake him, he does not budge.

Beneath the light of the moon, the junk is transformed and everything looks as if it might start to move at any second. The bus engine will start, the fan will begin to whirl, a piece of toast will pop out of the toaster, and the radio will begin to broadcast the news. Grandpa and I sing. The only song we both know is "Desert Moon," so we sing it again and again. The cats accompany us, yowling slightly off-key.

When the moon begins to set, I finally fall asleep. All three of us sleep soundly.

Eleven

After eating a breakfast of cookies and oranges, Grandpa goes home. He takes the blanket with him, saying, "It wouldn't do to have a cat make a nest in it," but he does not tell us to go home. Maybe it's the combination of lack of sleep, sitting scrunched up on the narrow seat, and the cold, but he walks slowly along the top of the embankment, his legs stiff like those of a rigid tin doll. From behind, he appears to have aged very suddenly.

The wind blows softly and the smell of grass is particularly strong today—the scent of spring that constricts my chest. Although it is the same this year as it was last spring, I feel that everything has changed since then. My grandmother, my father, my mother, and myself, the good little girl who always did well in school. And because it smells the same, the difference between last year and this seems even greater. Next year, wrapped within this same smell, what will I be feeling? A chill runs through me. "How many more times will Grandpa smell this smell?" The thought comes unbidden. I know that Grandpa must die someday, but until now it never occurred to me to wonder how much time he has left.

If you'd been younger, you wouldn't have been able to understand that sometimes it is better to die than to suffer. I can hear Grandpa's voice from last night in my mind. It was filled with satisfaction. And although it annoyed me for an instant because I myself am far from satisfied, I felt that there was no need to say anything more.

"Tomomi, the instant noodles are all gone." Tetsu is standing in the midst of a group of milling cats.

"Let's go," I say, and begin walking as though beating back the wind.

A man wearing a suit bursts out of the door beside the woman's apartment and rushes down the stairs. The man living next door to him comes out in coveralls and a hard hat and likewise runs down the stairs. Everyone is on their way to work. I am reminded of my father. The man in the suit smelled just like my father when he first wakes up in the morning.

"Maybe she's already left," Tetsu says, looking up at me. "We might have just missed her."

"But we came along the top of the embankment the whole way," I argue.

Her bicycle is still in exactly the same spot where she parked it that rainy night. I wonder what could have happened to her. No matter how many times we knock, she doesn't come to the door.

We decide to check out the factory, and start to head down the stairs. But just then we hear the sound of the door opening slightly.

"Oh, it's you." The woman is wearing faded blue pajamas with a flower print and her eyes are swollen. "So that's it. She was still asleep," I am thinking to myself just as Tetsu asks, with great concern, "Are you sick?"

"Naw, it's not that bad," she says, but her body is bent forward, as though just standing is painful.

"Did you go to the doctor?" Tetsu asks, going inside the door.

"No need for that. I've just got a bit of a fever, that's all."

I give Tetsu's shirt a yank to warn him that he is intruding, but she twists her body toward the stove in the kitchen.

"Can I ask you a favor?"

We have no time to ask what. She doubles over and crouches down on the linoleum floor.

"Ma'am?"

"I'm fine, fine," she mumbles, but her eyes remain closed. Her head, which seems very heavy, lolls forward to rest on the floor and her chest is heaving.

"*Ohhh!*" Tetsu cries in a voice like a balloon that has suddenly had the air let out, and he crouches down beside her.

I shove my arms under her armpits and start dragging her.

"It's all right. I've got you. I'm going to put you in bed, okay?" My mouth keeps moving of its own accord. "Tetsu, hurry. Pull back the quilt," I say, and he pulls it back slowly. When I have laid her down on the futon, he covers her gently as if afraid the weight of the quilt will crush her. Her ragged breathing, painful even to listen to, gradually eases, and then it seems that all the sweat in her body is pouring out.

Tetsu sits on his heels beside her, straight as a pin, and holds the palm of his hand above her nose. He keeps his hand still, not moving an inch.

"What're you doing? Practicing your ESP?"

"I'm making sure she doesn't stop breathing."

I snort and stand up. The towel in the washbowl beside her pillow is warm. I refill the washbowl with cold water at the kitchen sink, and then squeeze the excess water from the towel.

The large pot she uses for the cats is sitting on the range, filled with stewed fish scraps and cabbage. I stand with the lid in my hand and sigh.

It is all because she got soaked in the rain. Even for the cats, surely letting herself get sick is going too far. Like the contents of the pot in front of me, I am filled with a jumble of things—regret, anger, frustration. People are always talking about whether something is useful or not, about who is strong and who is weak, about who gets good marks or bad, about whether something is clean or dirty, yet at the same time they discard or ignore things that have become an inconvenience to them. No matter how hard the woman works, people will still abandon their cats, and they will continue to ignore NO DUMPING signs.

I place the cool, damp towel on her forehead, and she opens her eyes slowly. The sparsely lashed lids tremble slightly, and I see myself reflected in the narrow dark eyes that gaze out between them.

"Are you going to call the doctor?" Tetsu whispers, looking from one to the other of us.

"I'm all right. More important than me . . ." She pauses to shift her body slightly. "In the pot . . ."

"I know. I saw." We have no choice. "It's okay. We'll feed the cats for you," I say.

By the time we return to the apartment and have washed the bucket, dishpans, and plastic containers, it's already noon. "How was it?" the woman says, trying to sit up, but the color drains from her face, leaving it as white as a sheet of paper, and she lies back down.

"They were starving. I thought they wouldn't trust us, but they ate lots," Tetsu replies, and then turns to me. "Right, Tomomi? It went fine."

I grunt assent and sink down onto the floor. The bicycle was so heavy and wobbly with the bucket full of cat food on it that it was hard labor making the trip to the bus and the park, and then back again.

"There are some apples in the fridge. You eat them," the woman says in a hoarse voice.

I sit beside her pillow and begin peeling. The sound of the

117

knife sliding against the apple echoes strangely and I am so nervous I cut my finger.

"Oh! You're bleeding!" Tetsu wails. The woman opens her eyes.

"The drawer under the TV," she says.

I pinch Tetsu's arm surreptitiously. Stupid kid. Why did he have to make such a big fuss?

The woman sits up and peels the apple deftly. As I tape a bandage from the drawer on my cut, so small it practically stopped bleeding when I licked it, I am entranced by her hands. The knife moves as if by magic and the flesh of the apple, something I should be used to seeing, is round and plump like a marshmallow, a tennis ball, or a cream-filled bun. She peels two apples and cuts them into quarters on the palm of her hand.

"Here, shall I feed you?" Tetsu takes a piece of apple and pokes it against her lips.

"No, I don't need any."

"But you have to eat! If you don't, the doctor will give you a big, fat needle," he says gleefully. That is what Mother always says to him. "A big, fat needle." *Jab!*

The woman groans, glaring at the apple, then reluctantly takes a bite.

"Good?"

"Mmm."

"Then one more."

She eats two pieces of apple. After taking some medicine, she lies down, breathing with effort. She says, "I didn't have any appetite, but I guess it pays to try." Then her mouth tightens into a straight line. I think she's trying to smile.

I feel somewhat guilty because all I have done is cut my finger and eat the apple she peeled for us.

"I'll make supper for the cats," I tell her.

"You can cook, Tomomi?" Tetsu exclaims. I glare at him. He just blinks at me.

"Of course I can!"

The woman weakly turns her head on the pillow. "Are you sure?"

"Yes, I'm sure."

"There's two cabbages in the fridge. Just chop them up. And there's half a bag of dried sardines. You can use them all."

Oh, so you chop the cabbage, do you. I see. "And the sardines?" I ask.

"Put them in the pot with some water, and after you've boiled them a little add the cabbage. Be careful not to put in too much water. The cabbage is already watery," she says all in one breath, then is interrupted by a coughing fit that sounds painful. "Tomomi, are you sure you can do it?"

"No problem. She made instant noodles once," Tetsu answers for me, although I'm actually rather nervous.

There are now three bandages on my left hand: two for knife cuts, and one for a burn. It took me an hour and a half to chop the cabbage. The palm of my right hand is still cramped from gripping the knife for so long.

I wave my bandage-covered hand around. *"Look, Mom!"* I want to tell her. *"I made supper for the cats. And it was pretty popular, too."*

But my mother doesn't look at me. "I'm sorry about last night!" I blurt out, and then look at Grandpa, who nods, his mouth full of rice.

"That's okay. Did you have fun?" But her tone tells me it's not okay.

"It was great! The cats made a weird noise," Tetsu says, mimicking a high-pitched yowl.

My mother slips a piece of tofu from the miso soup into her mouth. She doesn't seem angry. It's more like she's saying, "I will feel nothing. Not even if you hit me, or pinch me . . ."

"Why don't you say something? I can tell you want to," I say to her after dinner when she's sitting in front of the TV. *"Mother!"* I yell silently. *"Look at me! Even if it is just to get mad at me."* I refuse to back down, wanting to destroy the transparent wall between us. "I said I was sorry!"

"It's not your fault." The eyes she turns to me are red. "I'm just a little tired, that's all."

She looks back at the TV, but I know she doesn't see anything. She is deeply depressed.

As I stand up wordlessly, she says, "Good night. You probably didn't get much sleep last night anyway, right?"

"Um. Good night." I say no more and trudge up the stairs. I should do something, but I have no idea what.

Twelve

The three kittens in the park are racing around in circles and pouncing on their mother's long tail. Lowering their heads and raising their rear ends, their tails curving, they creep up slowly and then leap with sudden force. Even when she appears to be sound asleep, the mother cat keeps them entertained by swishing her tail back and forth.

Sometimes they chase butterflies, but they haven't caught any yet. When we laugh at yet another failed attempt, one of the kittens turns toward us with a dazed expression and then pricks up its ears and lowers its head toward the key chain that Tetsu is dangling in front of its face. It seems to have completely forgotten the butterfly.

"Well, let's start cleaning up," I say, standing up from the bench where I have been sitting, and stretching like a cat. At this time of day I have usually only just gotten up. *"Erghh."* I stretch my arms and legs as far as they will go, and my remaining sleepiness leaves me.

When we checked in on the woman early this morning, she still had a fever. Tetsu and I balanced the cat food that we had made the day before on the bicycle and went first to the broken-down bus and then to the park. When Tetsu, watching the cats eat, remarks, "The way they eat reminds me of Grandpa," we both laugh. It's true. Grandpa's false teeth don't fit properly and he chews gingerly. The cats, too, turn their heads first to the right and then to the left, making a smacking noise and moving their jaws so much it makes me feel antsy.

"Look, Tomomi." I hear Tetsu's voice as I am collecting the dishes. I look behind and see a kitten clinging to the knee of his long corduroy trousers. "What should I do? I was playing around with him and he jumped on me."

Tetsu stands frozen, his left leg with the kitten attached completely rigid as if he is playing Red Light, Green Light. The kitten seems at a loss, too, just clinging desperately.

I squat down by his leg and gently lift off the kitten. His back is so incredibly thin beneath the soft fur that I am afraid to hold him. His claws, small yet sharp, are stuck in the cloth, which makes a ripping sound as I pull him off. He is the most active of the three kittens, and has a ring of black fur circling his nose that looks as if it has been drawn on. We call him Black Nose. He struggles a bit, trying to escape my hands.

"Don't be afraid," Tetsu says in a low voice, over and over, gently patting Black Nose's head between the flattened ears, and gradually the trembling beneath the soft fur begins to lessen. I feel him start to purr.

"He's saying that it feels good," Tetsu remarks, concentrating his whole being in his fingertips and continuing to pat Black Nose with a serious expression on his face. The kitten's ears, which looked as if they were stuck to his head, begin to relax, and I can see the pink skin inside them. Tetsu picks up Black Nose's front paw with his fingertips and waggles it gently as if shaking his hand. "Hi there."

Mimicking Tetsu, I shake Black Nose's paw. The bottom of the paw feels strange: dry and soft, yet taut. It is like nothing I have ever touched before.

Black Nose mews a little, as if responding to our greetings.

"My name is Tetsu Kiriki."

But Black Nose suddenly struggles and slips from my hands. Then he shoots like a bullet to where his mother is watching from the grass.

In the afternoon we go home to get our bicycles and then ride to the shopping center, which is quite far. We make the rounds to seven fish shops that have promised to give the woman their scraps every Friday. Today is Friday, and so we go for her.

"I'm sorry to make you do this, but they will be expecting me," she says, looking truly sorry as she hands us a piece of paper with a map to the shops.

All the shopkeepers know her and are worried when they hear that she is ill. Some say, "I didn't know she had children," and some give us candy. But not all of them.

"I hear she feeds the scraps to the strays. That's a problem, you know," the keeper of the last shop says, folding her arms. Her face is pointed like a barracuda's.

"Would it be wrong to feed them scraps?"

Barracuda walks in front of me, her rubber boots squeaking, and dumps a pail of dirty water from a plastic bucket. "After all, some of our paying customers have cats, too."

But at that moment, Tetsu, who has been looking in the window of the convenience store next door, bursts in. Completely ignorant, he shouts, "Thank you for the fish!" and Barracuda stares at him. "Cats really love fish, don't they? I don't like it much myself, although dried horse mackerel isn't so bad, I guess."

Shaking her head in exasperation, Barracuda goes into the back of the store and brings us a full plastic bag. Our bicycle carriers are filled with gifts for the cats.

When we return to the apartment, we wash the bloody scraps clean in the kitchen sink. I thought it would be so revolting that I would not be able to do it, but am surprised to find that when I set my mind to it, I have no problem at all.

Tonight's supper is nothing but fresh stewed fish scraps. The cats seem happier with this than with the usual vegetables and dried fish. *"Prrrrr,"* they rumble deep in their throats as they eat.

"Let's sleep over in the bus again sometime. If Mom doesn't like the idea, she can come and stay with us, too." Tetsu taps his fingertips against the bus, drumming out a rhythm, and looks back at me. The bus is dyed orange by the setting sun, almost as if it has been repainted. Tetsu is dyed, too. I am about to say, "Yes, let's," when someone calls out to us from behind.

"What're you doing?"

I turn around to see Kinko, a boy from my class. His fine hair is bobbed, and he is wearing a spotless white polo shirt. His narrow eyes flick suspiciously from the cats to our bicycles piled with buckets and containers. His mouth is gaping and his shiny lips look as if they are about to drool at any minute. Whenever I see him, I feel irritated. Although his last name is Kaneko, his nickname is Kinko, and he is the type of kid who cries when girls jeer, "Kinko, chinko," at him just because "chinko" is a slang word for penis.

Kinko puts the white curly-haired dog he is holding down on the ground, in front of the mountain of junk. When he removes the leash, a red one with a golden clasp, the dog begins yapping fearfully and running round and round in circles like an idiot. The cats scatter and Tetsu gives a cry, disappearing behind a fridge lying on its side.

"What are you doing in a place like this?" Kinko looks around, his mouth still slack. "That was your brother, I presume?"

"Yeah, so what?" You presume indeed. You jerk.

He wrinkles his nose at the bucket and repeats, "What are you doing?" He is always looking for a chance to snitch on someone.

I am about to snap, "Feeding the cats, as if it's any of your business," but at that moment a tabby cat with runny eyes rubs its stiff fur against my leg.

"Ew! What a filthy cat," Kinko exclaims, backing away. He

125

gives me a strange look, as if wondering how I can stand to let it touch me. He seems to be trying to keep from laughing.

"I don't mind," I mumble. It really is dirty.

"Ehhh!" he exclaims, and the enormous cat growls in response. Kinko takes another half step back. "There sure are a lot of strays around here."

"Looks like it." So why doesn't he tie up that stupid dog, I think.

"This is the first time I've been here." He purses his lips and pulls his eyebrows together as if pretending to think deeply. "It's because people feed them, that's what my mother says."

"Them? You mean the cats?"

"Yeah."

"Kinko, chinko. Are you stupid?"

Kinko is taken aback for an instant and his eyes dart about even more.

"People come here to throw their cats away. Wouldn't you say it's *their* fault that all these cats are here?"

"But—" Kinko pulls at the collar of his clean white polo shirt with a plump finger. "Don't people throw them away because they know someone will feed them?"

For a second I think that I have heard wrong. People throw their cats away because they know someone will feed them?

"That's what my mother says. The cats come here because people feed them. And because there are lots of cats here, people think it's okay to throw them away."

"Kinko, chinko."

"Stop calling me that."

"Kin-ko-chin-ko." I open my mouth wide and enunciate very clearly. "So would you throw a cat away as long as there was food for it to eat?"

"My dad hates cats, so we would never have one in the first place." He shakes his bobbed head vigorously. I know that my eyes are hard and bright.

Kinko's eyes meet mine and he looks about hastily, calling "Lulu!" inanely. There is no need to shout. The dog is right beside him.

"Well, bye." He picks up the dog and starts climbing clumsily up the bank.

"Now, just a minute! Then what are you saying we should do? Let them starve to death? Or maybe we should bring along some poison gas!"

"Don't ask me. I don't know," he says, in a voice near tears. "But my mother says the cats here are dirty. She says if you touch them you'll get sick."

The tabby cat at my feet is diligently licking his bottom. I pick him up and press his runny-eyed face right under Kinko's nose.

"Eek!"

Kinko runs away. With my arm under his front legs, the cat dangles down, incredibly long. He is about twice as long as when he is sitting down.

"Come back here! Why don't you touch him and see if it's really true that you'll get sick!"

"No!" The dog is barking excitedly, clutched in Kinko's arms as he runs. What an idiot. He doesn't know what he is talking about. He just repeats whatever his mother says.

127

The cat, which has been waving his legs frantically, twists from my arms and drops to the ground. He blinks rapidly and then glares at me.

"Sorry," I say.

He shakes himself and all his fur stands on end, but then he begins licking his front paw as though nothing has happened.

"Phew! Are you ever heavy! Shall we try that again?" But he twists his back like a snake and stalks lazily away.

Tetsu's eyes have been crossed for the last few minutes.

"If you can't read it, give it to me."

"It's okay." He turns his back, and his eyes become even more crossed as he grunts with the effort of concentration.

"One hundred point two!" he finally announces in a loud voice, and then lets out a deep breath. "Your fever's gone down a lot."

The woman nods rather bashfully as if he has just read her the figures on a weight scale. Then she bows deeply, saying, "Really, thank you so much. I mean, it's been . . ."

"Four days since you got the fever," I answer, shaking the thermometer. It's hard to believe that not even a week has passed since we spent the night in the bus.

"Really! I never thought it would last so long. I never get sick."

I make noodles with egg for lunch. There are some green onions in the fridge, so I try chopping them up. It's easier than chopping cabbage. Then all I do is drop an egg (plus a little eggshell) into the instant noodles. I have chopped the onions too coarsely and they have a rather sharp taste, but it feels good to be sitting in the sun-filled room, the three of us eating together, particularly when I have made the meal myself. I can make cat food and noodles. Even though that is all I can cook, I feel that I could live anywhere in the world.

"Did you know that cats sneeze? They yawn and cough, too," Tetsu says when he has drunk the last drop of his soup. "Not only that, but cats have different cries. When they pester me to feed them, one of them goes like this, '*Ennh-ennh*,' while another one goes '*Aanng-aang*.'"

"I know, I know. The one who goes '*Aanng-aang*' is the brown tabby, right?" Finishing her noodles, the woman piles her bowl on top of mine and rubs the palm of her hand over her face, which is still pale and dry.

"Yeah, that cat starts yowling '*Aang-aang*' from far away, but then when it reaches us, instead of digging into the food, it always sharpens its claws on everything in sight first." Tetsu wipes his nose on his sleeve. "I wonder why eating noodles makes people's noses run? I'll have to look it up in a book later."

"It's like he is saying, 'Hooray! It's chow time. *Rrripp*!'" I say, and the woman laughs.

"I'm going to feed them myself today," she declares and claps her hands together loudly. I think she has missed them.

"Hi there."

Hearing someone call me, I turn to see Black Nose standing in the doorway. He is wearing blue shorts and standing primly. "Hi, Tomomi."

He can talk? A cat? His nose with its little circle of black fur

129

quivers. "Don't stare at me like that. It makes me nervous. Can I come in?"

"Sure," I say, hastily.

"Hmm. It's nice and tidy." He takes off his sneakers and steps onto the linoleum of the kitchen floor. He looks around him. The fur on his slightly protruding chest is the same as always, a little longer than the rest of his fur and sticking up.

"Tomomi."

"Yeah?"

"You like it here, don't you?"

"Yes, I do."

"So you won't be going back home again, will you?"

I start in surprise and wake up. I have fallen asleep sitting on the chair in the woman's kitchen with my forehead pressed against the refrigerator, waiting for the water in the pot to boil.

The kitchen is full of steam. Where can Tetsu be? I switch off the stove and turn around. The woman is sleeping with her back toward me, her body rounded with her head and its tightly permed curls buried in her chest. It reminds me of the way Tetsu sleeps.

Her temperature has risen again. She probably won't be able to feed the cats tonight, I think, and look around the apartment. I like it here. Always neat and orderly, with plenty of sunshine. It has a good feeling, like a room that has been well kept for a long time. The brightly polished pots and stove. The sheets, repeatedly washed and ironed. The tidy fridge. The white soap placed on the small washstand. When I'm here, I feel that nothing bad can happen. There is not one thing missing. Just the woman, Tetsu, the cats, and me. This is all that comprises the world.

So why did I have that dream? Naturally I go home every day. When he said, "So you won't be going back home again, will you?" it shocked me. As if I had been asked a question I didn't want to answer.

I walk carefully so as not to make a sound and stand before a small picture frame on top of the dresser. The photograph shows a boy, perhaps a little older than Tetsu, wearing blue shorts. He is in someone's garden. There is a large spirea tree in full bloom. The boy is squinting as if it is too bright, gazing up at the eaves of a house in the corner of the picture. At first I think he is just looking up, but when I examine it more closely I see that there is a cat on the roof mewing at the boy, as if trying to tell him something.

The woman rolls over and I turn my eyes away from the photograph. I wonder who that boy is. I noticed this picture yesterday but have been pretending not to see it. Tetsu is too short to see the top of the dresser, and I have not mentioned it to him.

I know nothing about this lady—why she feeds the cats, why she has no family . . . I know none of these things. What I do know is that she likes apples and hates milk, and that her name is Noriko Sasaki. I had to learn that from the address on her water bill because her apartment has no name plate, only the number 201 on the door. And I know one more thing. Sometimes in her sleep, she says, "Yotchan, I'm sorry."

When I first heard her say that, I felt very uncomfortable. I realized that although I like her, I never once wanted to know anything about her—despite the fact that many different things must have happened in her life, some bad, some sad, some secret even. But somewhere in my heart I wanted her to stay just the way that Tetsu and I know her: the woman who feeds the cats.

I turn and look at the boy in the photograph once again. "Let me stay here a little longer," I want to say to him. "My mother is still depressed and my father has not come home. And this woman still has a slight fever."

But the boy just looks at the cat and smiles.

Thirteen

I am the one who suggests that we go to our father's apartment the next day. If he isn't going to come back to us, then we will go to him. Instead of waiting, we can try asking him to come home. I wonder why I never thought of it before.

"Do you think it's okay? To show up without telling him?" Tetsu asks.

"He hasn't come home for nearly two weeks. What if he's died of starvation?"

"Dad will be furious if we interrupt his work."

"It'll be okay." Clutching the piece of paper with his address written on it, I follow the directions we were given by a policeman and turn at the corner by a row of used cars. With prices taped to their windshields, the silent cars stare at us as we pass by. Although we have come only five train stops from our house, it feels like a very long way.

"Aha! Isn't that it?"

"Which one?"

"That one, over there." Tetsu is pointing at an old two-story apartment building on the other side of a cabbage field. A sign with letters that look as if they have been written with a calligraphy brush bears the name SUNFLOWER APARTMENTS. So that is why the policeman said, "You can't miss it." Surrounded by brand-new apartment buildings, the old, yellowing mortar of its walls stands out plainly.

As we approach, I see that it is even more dilapidated than it appeared from a distance, and I am disappointed. We remove our shoes at the entrance and find that there are three rooms on either side of the corridor. It is like a dormitory, with a lot of rooms off a main hallway. There is a toilet on one side and a gas burner on the other side of the stairs at the end of the corridor, and a man wearing sweatpants stands with his back to us cooking something. His sweatpants are sagging a little, and I can see his checkered underwear. The whole place is permeated with the smell of cooking oil.

"You want something?" Sweatpants turns to look at us. He has a thick wad of cotton on his nose held in place with a bandage. While Tetsu stares at it, I hurriedly ask, "Is there a Mr. Kiriki living here?"

"Kiriki?" He turns off the gas, and the sizzling sound from the frying pan gradually dies away, like air slowly fizzling out of a balloon. Grabbing his slipping sweatpants with one hand,

134

he points with his chin. "Isn't that his room? You mean the college professor, right? The one who wears glasses."

My father does wear glasses, but he is not a professor. People often mistake him for one, though, maybe because of his unkempt hair that's just starting to turn white and his hunched shoulders.

"I think that must be him. He isn't a professor, though."

"Hmm." He turns toward us, carrying the frying pan. Sausages. Is he having supper at four in the afternoon?

"He's a translator. He translates from German into Japanese."

"Then that must be him." Sweatpants points to the door immediately on my left and starts climbing up the stairs, his slippers flapping. "He might be sleeping. He seems to stay up all night."

Stealthily putting my hand to the wooden door, I find it unlocked. Peeking through the crack, I can see someone lying on the tatami mats in the gloom. It is a woman. Careful not to make a sound, I hastily close the door. "It's not this room."

"Yes it is." Tetsu puts his fingers on the handle. I grasp his hand hard.

"No it's not."

"Why not?"

Why not? Because why would there be a woman sleeping in our father's room? I feel like everything is going black before my eyes. What will our mother do if she finds out? That would be the end. They would get a divorce, and Tetsu and I would be abandoned.

"But Mom's in there."

"Huh?"

There is a muddy shoe cupboard beside the entranceway. Its door is open, and Tetsu points to it. Beige pumps. Mom's dress shoes. He's right. It really is her.

Opening the door once more, softly, we go inside. Our mother is sound asleep, breathing gently, with both hands between her knees.

Tetsu's nostrils quiver. "Phew, it stinks," he whispers. "She's wearing perfume!"

But what is she doing here? Does she come often? There is a small desk by the window with books piled all around it. At the foot of the sink right beside the door is a futon folded in half. A pile of neatly folded laundry lies on top of the only cushion in the room. I take another look at our mother.

She is wearing a pale yellow dress. A dress that she bought with our father a long time ago, one that she wears only when we go out to eat at a restaurant or for special occasions. Those beige pumps, too. She has dressed herself up and put on perfume just to bring Dad his clean laundry.

I pull a blanket out from the folded futon and put it over her. She snuggles down inside it. I think she might wake up, but she doesn't budge.

When we get outside, Tetsu, who has followed me silently up until then, bursts out loudly, "Why did you do that? Are we going home already?"

"Let's leave it up to Mom for today."

She must have come here resolved to ask our father to return home. If she came intending to fight with him, she wouldn't have brought his laundry, and she certainly wouldn't have dressed up.

"Where's Dad? He's going to be surprised when he sees Mom." Tetsu turns back toward the apartment, aims his finger toward the closed window, and pretends to shoot it with a pistol.

"He'll be back soon." And if not, I think, he'd receive the death sentence after Mom had gone to so much trouble to make peace. "Oh, I wish I were a man."

"Why?" Tetsu reaches down to pick something up and walks along rubbing it against the sign for a pharmacy that stands between the cabbage field and the road.

"Because men have it easier."

"Why?"

"Quit asking why, why. I'm going," and I start to run.

Tetsu walks along the white line that floats distinctly against the dusky road as if on a balance beam. When we got off the train, we headed for the woman's apartment. This morning her legs still seemed rather wobbly but she did feed the cats. If we hurry, we should be in time to help give them supper.

"A long time ago, a really long time ago, there was a great thief who was able to escape in the pitch dark by using a stick. He swung the stick back and forth, and even though he couldn't see a thing, he was able to run at full speed."

Tetsu's face is dead serious, as if someone has told him he will die if he veers off the white line. Pitch darkness—I wonder what it feels like.

"Pretty amazing, isn't it? To be able to run when you can't see just by using a stick."

Yeah. I need a stick like that myself. When everything around me seems all blurred and confused and I can't move . . .

Tetsu stops. Some leather shoes approaching from the other direction are walking on the same white line. The shoes stop for a second, then continue until they are almost on top of Tetsu, pass swiftly around him, and step back onto the line.

"Tomomi, what's wrong?"

I stand as if frozen to the spot. It's him. Today he is wearing some kind of raincoat, but there is no doubt. It is the man in the gray coveralls with the gleaming eyes.

"What happened?" Tetsu comes back to where I am standing.

"Nothing." I continue walking, and when I look back, no one is there. The same as last time. When I looked back he was gone, and it started to rain . . .

"That guy." Tetsu looks back and tilts his head. "We met him before, didn't we?"

"Where?" I can barely manage to gasp out the word.

"That time it rained." Tetsu starts walking backward. "I remember because I was looking at his head and thinking he sure has a lot of hair."

"You did not. You didn't see anything." My voice is hoarse. How could he have when he was so oblivious that he didn't even notice what happened?

"I did too! Really, I saw."

"You didn't see anything!" Suddenly I am screaming. The words leap from my mouth like living things. "That man, he touched me! Here!" I point to my breast.

After that I grit my teeth, while the scream in my throat forms a lump that races violently back and forth between my stomach and my mouth.

Tetsu's pale-colored eyes gaze absently into space, then turn hard and black as if an ink stain has spread over them. I stare fixedly at his eyes as if at some strange new phenomenon. They remind me of something. Yes, that's it. A video I saw in science class of an eclipse of the sun. What am I thinking of? My body is still shaking. My muscles contract of their own accord.

The next instant Tetsu starts running. At first I don't understand what he's doing, but then suddenly I know and run after him.

"No!" I grab him from behind and hold him. He waves his arms and legs wildly. I screw my eyes shut and cling to him, even though he's kicking me and pulling my hair.

"Let me go! What are you doing? Let me go!"

"No! You can't!"

If you go, he will kill you. He will surely tear you to pieces quicker than he grabbed my breast. Even now, just that one glance at him has made everything go dark, as if he is some magician with a sinister smile swinging a great black cape. Everything, the cats, my father—they have all vanished to the far, far ends of the universe.

139

"Tomomi . . ." Tetsu is gasping. "You just don't think I could do it. You think he would beat me up!" He glares at me as if it is I, not that man, who has done something wrong. I have never seen Tetsu so angry before.

Fourteen

A hairy paw with shining claws, a dead cat, my mother's eyes swollen from weeping, rain pouring down, Tetsu's white face, a wall towering above . . . Like a blinking light, images flash before my eyes. All these things I destroy. Every time I move, every time I raise my voice to scream, everything I see is ripped to shreds, pulverized, or consumed by flames. I smash the wall, the bridge, the house. I smash the whole town. It feels wonderful. When I crush someone beneath my heel, I want to laugh uproariously. I will laugh as hard as I can. I feel restless and irritable, like before a sneeze.

Tomomi . . .

A hole suddenly gapes in my restlessness.

Tomomi . . .

Tetsu's white face is peering at me. "Are you all right? You were grinding your teeth like crazy."

My body is as stiff as a board. A roaring noise still reverberates in my brain, and when I let out my pent-up breath, my forehead throbs. Although I have had many similar dreams, none of them have felt so good, and that makes me nervous.

"The cats at the bus, there's something wrong with them," Tetsu stammers out.

"Something wrong?"

"Their fur is falling out."

"Is that all?" Has Tetsu just noticed that now? They were mangy old cats to start off with; a lot of them have bald patches and runny eyes.

"I talked with the lady this morning. I was worried, so I stopped by again on my way home . . ."

The words "on my way home" remind me. Tetsu started school again today. Which means that the junior-high entrance ceremony is tomorrow. For some reason, it's always held a day after elementary school begins.

Yesterday I went straight home. Tetsu said, "I'm going to see the cats," and I had watched him walk away alone, then ran home to find my junior-high-school uniform hanging in the wardrobe. My mother must have gone and got it for me. I closed the wardrobe door quickly and crawled into bed. And this morning when Tetsu left, I pretended to be asleep.

Well, I had better stop complaining about my headache and try on the uniform. I wonder if Mom got me some new socks to go with it. Although I have done my best to avoid it, I know, whether I like it or not, I will become a junior-high-school student. Whether I like it or not, I will grow up, and whether I like it or not . . .

But I have this strange feeling that somehow I will not be attending the entrance ceremony tomorrow. I wonder why . . .

". . . That's what she said." Tetsu's voice stops, and I come to my senses with a start.

"What did she say?"

"I just told you. She said it got worse suddenly. Even Blackie. He was there last night, though." We had started giving more of the cats names. Blackie was the big black tomcat that liked to sleep on the front seat of the bus.

I try to remember when it was that Blackie hadn't come to eat. I thought he hadn't come because the woman hadn't been with us . . .

"Half of his face was all scabby. And he didn't have much appetite when he ate." Tetsu falls silent.

"Aren't they eating?"

"Some of them aren't."

I am about to suggest taking them to the veterinarian but stop, amazed at my own stupidity. That would be impossible, of course. There are way too many of them, and besides, they would never sit still for a doctor.

As if he has read my thoughts, Tetsu says, "I bought some medicine at the pet shop," and climbs down the ladder of the bunk bed. He takes a brown bottle from a paper bag on the desk and climbs back up. He opens a book entitled *A Veterinarian's Guide to Cat Diseases and Their Treatment* and shows it to me. The page, marked by a piece of paper, has a note written beneath a photograph of a cat with a skin disease and the name of some medicine.

"You have to thin it with water and pour it over the cat. You shouldn't touch the medicine with your bare hands, that's what the man in the store told me."

"It sounds like some kind of poison." The bottle has a green top and is filled with a thick dark syrup.

"No problem. I got an old watering can from Grandpa."

"You're going to sprinkle it over them with a watering can?"

He nods. "It leaked, so Grandpa soldered it for me."

"Really?"

"All you have to do is ask Grandpa. He has everything."

"Except that most of it is old junk." But that old box for the sweet citron buns now serves as a peaceful resting place for a dead cat.

"I'm going to take them the medicine now. Do you want to come?"

"My head hurts."

"Do you want me to bring you an ice pack?"

"No, thanks."

I can't look him in the face when he says goodbye and turns away.

Tetsu. He tried to go after that man. For my sake. But even so, I am still afraid to go outside. I try to tell myself that it can't be helped. After all, my head really does hurt. But I know that it is because I lack courage.

Last night in the bathtub I looked down at my chest and started to tremble. My right breast has grown bigger, though just a little. But my left one, the one he touched, hasn't grown at all. It was only a single moment in time. I should just forget it. But no matter how often I tell myself that, my left breast still remains shrunken. After all those times when I wished that I would never grow taller, when I hoped that my legs would never get any longer, my flat left breast seems so miserable in comparison with the plump right one. I never meant for it to become numbed and frozen like this. All I wanted was to stay the way I was before, my old happy self.

Pressing my cool palm against my forehead, I climb out of bed. Looking down from the window, I see that Tetsu has already come out of the house. He is wearing rubber boots and has a rubber glove on one hand, in which he grasps the bottle of medicine. In the other he carries the watering can, filled to the brim, and he staggers along in the wind. There is no place to get water along the way. At this rate it will take him half an hour to reach the bus stop.

I look at the door to our room, which Tetsu has left open. Beyond that is the hallway, and through the window, which is open about four inches, I can hear the sound of the old man's tree clippers trimming branches next door.

I press my forehead against the cold glass window, through the worn lace curtain. At the corner Tetsu puts the heavy tin watering can on the ground, picks it up in his other hand, and begins walking again. The weight of the can pulls him forward, as if he is being dragged along on the tips of his toes. Then he vanishes behind the fragrant olive tree on the corner.

The instant he disappears from sight I realize I can't go back to bed. Like a person who has just regained consciousness, I feel a million questions race through my mind. Yet I have known the answers all along. More than that man, more than my breasts about which I have been so concerned, what really matters is the fact that the cats are sick. What on earth was I thinking, hiding inside the house like this?

"Tetsu. Wait," I whisper in a small voice and, returning slowly to my dresser, I begin to change. I have to go. I have to go today. Because the cats are sick. The cats, which I hadn't realized I'd come to care about, are sick.

"Are you going out?" I'm crouching down in the entrance hall when Grandpa calls out to me from behind. "Hey! Tomomi."

"Mmm," I mumble. When I reached the bottom of the stairs everything turned bright yellow.

"Look at you. Your face is so pale."

I'm about to say that I can't go after all when I hear a dry sound like a bird folding its wings and without thinking I look around. "It's Grandma," I tell myself. "Grandma didn't die. I've just been dreaming all this."

But that's because of the fan that Grandpa holds open in his hand. A faint fragrance wafts from its faded blue folds. Grandma's smell.

I take the fan and press my face against it. The soft smell spreads and the feel of Grandma's hand against my cheek, my forehead, returns to me. Grandma brushing my hair, cleaning my ears, finding me when I was lost, holding my hand—her own soft and dry, always covered with fine wrinkles; her hand smelled good.

"If you want it, you can have it."

"Did you find it in the storage room?"

He nods and then says again, "You look awful. Did you take your temperature?"

"When did she buy it?"

"Hmmm." Grandpa falls deep into thought.

But it doesn't really matter. I am in a state of shock. I had felt Grandma here with such certainty. It was so sudden, so vivid. And that feeling, which I have not felt since she died, a feeling that I thought I had lost forever, did not drop down upon me from some far, unreachable place but came from somewhere deep within my own being. That is what surprises me most of all.

I gently close the fan. "Would you put it on my desk for me? I have to hurry."

"Are you sure you're all right?"

"Yes. I feel a bit better now."

"Okay, then," and he puts his shoes on and opens the door for me. A warm moist breeze blows in.

"Did you finish with the organ?"

"Yup. I couldn't fix it." He shrugs. "I put it out in the storage shed."

I thank him for the fan and dash out under the sky, where the clouds race with tremendous speed.

The wind, which has been pushing me along from behind, suddenly becomes an invisible wall blocking my way. It blows wild and fitfully, gradually increasing in strength. I walk along slowly, as if carrying a fragile egg inside my head. But the pain does not seem so bad in the wind.

When I finally reach the broken bus, Tetsu isn't there. My strength spent, I squat down on the ground. Feeling a small presence behind me, I turn to find Blackie. Half of his face has gone bald, just as Tetsu said.

"Did he treat you with the medicine?" When I reach out my hand, he backs away and mews silently. As if he's on the TV screen with the sound turned off, his mouth opens but I can't hear anything. He has lost his voice. He opens and closes his mouth several times and then gives up and goes into the bus.

I walk quietly so as not to startle the cats, peering softly into cracks and corners. It is true that their shedding has gotten much worse. Some of them have pink patches of flesh poking through their fur like islands on a map of the ocean, and the ears of some are completely naked, while the skin of even those that are not so badly affected has grown dry all over. If only we had noticed sooner.

"From now on, I'll come every day and bring you medicine, okay?" I tell each one of them, feeling it may already be too late.

Someone must have come to dump garbage again. I find a motorbike with its tires gone, looking like the bones of a dinosaur. The cat curled up on its seat is new here, too. It cries mournfully, a long-drawn-out cry, as if it's calling someone. I approach slowly, and it opens its eyes wide with fright, then leaps from the seat to hide among the scraps of sheet metal.

Where is Tetsu? At that moment I stub my foot on something. A watering can. A sturdy old tin watering can. Picking it up, I see that it gleams darkly wet inside. It must be Tetsu's. But why did he just leave it here, as if he tossed it away in a hurry?

Suddenly I am worried.

Tetsu isn't at the park either. I should never have let him come alone. An unpleasant possibility begins to fill my mind.

Tetsu must have met that man again.

And if he did, he probably went for him all by himself. I remember Tetsu's eyes yesterday.

When the cats realize I haven't brought any food they scatter in disappointment. Only Black Nose and his siblings play about at my feet, clawing at my socks.

"Was Tetsu here? Was he?" Black Nose struggles in my hands when I pick him up. "Tell me. If he came, mew once. If not, mew twice. Okay?"

But instead of mewing, he scratches my thumb.

"Ouch!" Falling nimbly to the ground, Black Nose tears off. I stare stupidly at the thin red-stained scratch, then rub it vigorously.

Wait a minute. Why am I so uneasy and afraid? Tetsu might just have gone down to the river to play. But no matter how I reason with myself, I can't get rid of my anxiety. My headache gradually returns.

If I just stand here, I'll get even more anxious, so, without knowing where I'm going, I start walking. When I reach the crossroads where we saw the man yesterday, my vision darkens for an instant, but I force myself to go on. An old man taking his dog for a walk appears and then a man wearing a suit. I stare after them until all that is left is dust swirling in the wind. Alone, I start walking again past houses that seem cold and indifferent. And I remember an incident that the cats at the dump with their patches of baldness have jogged in my memory.

It happened when Tetsu was five years old. My father always cut Tetsu's hair with a pair of electric hair clippers, but he did it so clumsily that the end result looked like rows of close-cropped ridges. This particular time was even worse than usual. He had made three round bald patches, like coins. My mother was furious and snatched the clippers away while my father was still cutting, and the result was another bald spot. Tetsu, his eyes swollen from crying, had given up resisting and just sat there, as if deaf to the two of them yelling at each other right over his head. When I saw him I burst into tears. It was just too much. Not only was his head shaved in zigzags, but on top of that my parents were shoving him around. They fell silent and Tetsu blinked his eyes fiercely, saying over and over again, "I'm okay. I'm okay." And then, when I finally stopped crying, he handed me his favorite stuffed toy, an alligator, saying, "Here, you can have it."

Walking along, I suddenly laugh to myself. It seems funny now. I feel a little guilty that those poor sick cats have reminded me of such a thing. Still . . . although my parents sometimes had spectacular fights, it was different in those days.

Turning the corner, I enter the street in front of our house.

At first I think I am hearing things. A thin, wailing voice. Tetsu's voice. When I realize that it is coming from the garden next door, I run into our yard and climb frantically up onto the wall.

At first I don't understand what's going on. My anxiety is making me see things, I think. The old man next door is clutching Tetsu's arm and trying to drag him over to the incinerator in the corner of the yard. "Now I've got you. What were you going to do with that, huh?"

I see that Tetsu is holding a cat that looks like a dirty rag.

"You were going to do it again, weren't you? You little brat!"

The old man must have been going for a walk because he is carrying his walking stick and tries to poke the cat while Tetsu twists away, protecting it.

I think at first that the old man is right, that Tetsu has brought another dead cat to put in his yard. But though the cat is hanging limply, at that moment it moves. It struggles weakly in his arms, its hair falling out and its eyes half-closed.

"He's sick." Tetsu's voice is a shrill falsetto. "Let me go. He's really sick. I have to help him."

"Tell the truth. Say that it was you who put those dead cats in here."

"I don't know anything about it. I was taking him to my house. You're the one who dragged me into your yard."

"Listen here." The old man shakes Tetsu, drawing him close. "If there's one thing I can't stand, it's a liar."

At those words, a switch inside Tetsu suddenly flips.

151

"Liar? You're the liar!" His face, his whole body are contorted. "Yes, it was me. I did it. Because you're mean, because you're a dirty old liar, that's why I did it!"

"Why, you—!"

The old man raises the stick in his blue-veined hand. Tetsu's face is drained of blood, his thin arm clutched by the man.

I hear a terrible scream coming from far away. But it is I, straddling the top of the wall, who am screaming.

As long as I live, I will never forget the face the old man turned to me. With his stick still raised vigorously toward the sky, his expression is neither angry nor surprised. There is not even a trace of shame. He merely looks at me with an expressionless mask that shows only slight annoyance, while my scream goes on and on, as if I am letting out everything that I've been keeping inside.

Now, before your very eyes, yes, I *will* become a monster. The nightmare that I have seen again and again, I will make it come true for you. I no longer want to be good. It doesn't matter that our father is gone. If someone touches me again, I will no longer be hurt or afraid. So, God, please, make me a monster. I don't care if I can never come back. I don't care if I die. Here, now, just for one second of time make me terrifying. Before the eyes of this man who dares to harm Tetsu, make me the scariest thing in the world.

At that moment I know at last what the scariest thing in the world is. Hate.

All I remember is seeing a flash of light running through the old man's eyes. A flash of hatred—my hatred for him reflected back at me. Then Tetsu is grabbing my ankle where I sit on top of the wall, my eyes squeezed firmly shut, and shaking it, saying, "Tomomi! Tomomi!" Looking up at me with his nose running and his face covered with tears, he is hiccuping. I jump down onto the muddy ground.

The thin old man lies like a shriveled corpse on the cold earth of the garden, his stick still clutched in his hand.

"What happened?"

Tetsu begins to shake and grabs on to me. "He just fell over all of a sudden."

"Are you okay?"

"Yes," he answers, and then bursts into tears again.

It's getting dark. Maybe his wife has gone out shopping; there is no light on in the house. If we leave him like this, he will die. At least, he probably will . . . But even if he does, it's not my fault. It's not anybody's fault. Besides, who cares if someone like him dies, anyway?

The wind sweeps past me, and when I look around, my house seems terribly far away. By now, surely, there must be a light shining from the storage room window. But I can't see it from here. I don't know why, but I suddenly feel I may never go home.

I look once again at the old man, lying there. Then back at my house. Then suddenly my heart is still, as if it has been completely wrapped in cotton, and I realize that I am standing at a very dangerous crossroads. A crossroads where, if I make the wrong choice, I will never be able to return.

Grandpa. Now I finally understand why he spends all his time tidying up the storage room. Our house is full of treasure. Dusty, long-forgotten treasures. And Grandpa wants Tetsu, me, my father, and most of all my mother to remember those treasures. That is why he tried to fix the organ. That is why he gave me the fan. He wants to tell us, we who are in danger of falling apart, that this is our home.

Home. I want to go home.

I place my foot on the cherry tree, climb over the wall, and jump down into our yard by the clothesline. I hit my knee badly, but feel no pain. I race past the side of the shed, open the back door, and kick off my shoes. When I was little, if I got lost all I had to do was cry. Wherever I went, someone was there to take me by the hand. But now it's different.

Inside, it is completely dark. It feels as if I'm wading through water, but I do not falter, nor do I bump into anything. Standing in front of the telephone in the living room, I pick up the receiver and dial the three-digit number I have always known but never used until now.

"Hello. We need an ambulance." After giving the next-door neighbor's name and address, I replace the receiver. The sounds of the world that had been stilled gradually return.

I crumple to the floor.

Fifteen

When I disappeared over the wall—my eyes, according to Tetsu, glazed over like those of someone who had just seen a mirage in the desert—Tetsu stood there, stunned, forgetting even to cry. Then, still holding the limp cat in his arms, he poked our unconscious neighbor fearfully with one finger. The old man did not move. He was about to poke him again when suddenly he heard a cry from behind. The man's wife was sitting on the ground with the contents of her shopping basket spilled all around her. She grabbed on to Tetsu, who had raced unthinking to her side, and tried to stand, but her small feet in their gray shoes kept slipping in the mud and she clutched Tetsu's waist even tighter. Struggling to help her up,

Tetsu himself fell down. Then the ambulance came, taking the old man and his wife, and leaving Tetsu all alone.

All this I hear later from Tetsu, when I'm in my hospital bed. The only thing I vaguely remember is that it was Grandpa who lifted me from where I lay beside the telephone. After that I developed a very high fever and was hospitalized the next day. Oblivious, not even dreaming, I slept deeply and didn't open my eyes until the morning of the fourth day. This, too, I learn only later.

That morning I wake in a strange white room filled with golden light. I feel a wonderful sensation of soft fluid, like some kind of nectar, coursing slowly through my body. The bright sky spreads out beyond the window, and the cherry trees are in full bloom. The piercing clarity of birds singing as they flit, almost dancing among the trees, pervades every inch of me.

In a chair by the window, my mother sleeps. Her hair is disheveled and her face is without makeup except for a small trace of lipstick. She is nodding slowly, like someone rocking in a boat. "Mom," I try to say, but no sound comes out. Still, I am content.

"The cat I brought home has a big fat tail, so I named him Tail. At first Mom said no, but then she said I can keep him until he recovers as long as he's the only one. He's getting a little better. He was so cold he shivered all over, so I got an old blanket from Grandpa and wrapped him up in it. Then Grandpa told me that I should mix some protein powder with milk and feed him. When I was little, I didn't drink much milk, so that's what he used to do for me, he said. But I can't mix in too much. Tail hates the way it smells and won't drink it if I do."

As I doze on and off, I feel Tetsu's words flow inside of me like small, flickering flames. One day, he paces around and around my bed, softly touching the quilts, and announces as if to himself, "When the cats get better, Tomomi will, too."

At first I can't speak. I wonder whether I will ever be able to speak again, but the thought doesn't really bother me. My mother and father peer anxiously into my face and talk to me as if I am a little baby, which makes me want to laugh.

It is an almost disappointingly ordinary thing that gets me talking again. One evening, after my father, my mother, and Tetsu have gone home to eat, Grandpa appears unexpectedly in my room. He has never asked any questions about why Tetsu was in the garden next door or why I collapsed by the telephone, but I have a feeling that he knows somehow, without asking. With his plump, warm hand, he ruffles my bangs, which are longer now and lie flat across my forehead, and says, "The next-door neighbor came home today." "Oh, good, he didn't die," I think to myself, and before I realize it, tears are rolling down my cheeks one after the other. The ice in my heart melts, and I feel something beginning to flow like melting snow. Grandpa looks at me and nods his head, then opens up the parcel he has brought with him. Inside, along with some books and snacks, is Grandma's fan.

It must have been Grandma who protected me. When I think of what might have happened if the old man had died, my heart goes cold. And I think that the reason he did not die

157

is that Grandma put in a word for me with God. People, cats, every living thing must die sometime. Like a piece of wood bobbing with the ebb and flow of the tide near the shore—weak, unreliable—someday we will finally be washed away by the waves.

I am sure that Grandma is watching over me. For now I remember. When I was little, I often flew into a temper and cried, and it was Grandma who told me, "Tomomi, you are special. You try to communicate everything inside of you with absolute honesty. Only that is not such an easy thing to do, is it?"

I didn't really understand what she meant and consequently I forgot it for a long time. But she is the only one who ever said that to me. I gently grasp the fan.

"Do you want some apple?"

I nod and Grandpa opens the drawer in the nightstand beside the bed. "Now, where is the knife?"

"In the red bag," I say in a small voice.

It is a Saturday in mid-July, the day our final tests are over. I sit with the woman near the minibus on a sofa with a spring popping out, watching the cats.

I have not seen her for three months. I began going to school again in May, more than a month after the school year had started, so I had to work very hard to catch up. And I've had tennis club practices almost every day after school, and matches on Sundays.

"So that means you've been working hard," she says. Her

face is shining with sweat. "You've gotten very tan. And that hairstyle. I didn't recognize you at first."

"Does it look funny?" I pull a tuft of hair on the top of my head between my fingers. "I mean, look how short it is."

"No, it's not funny. It suits you."

"And I've gotten fat, too. A little."

"You can't call that fat!" She shakes her head. "You look more like a girl, that's all. And that's good! Very good!"

She says the latter so emphatically that we both burst out laughing.

It has been a long time. I look up at a silver jet plane slowly crossing the bright blue sky. The gray sky and strong wind of spring are gone. Even the noise of the expressway sounds different. Everything seems to have happened so long ago.

"This sofa, it was thrown away—let's see—last month, I think. At first it was in good shape. I wanted to take it home with me, but I can't drive. And now look at it. It's already like this." She tries to push the spring sticking out of a rip back under the cloth.

"There's less than half the number there used to be," I remark, looking at the cats eating their dinner.

"It was awful," she says, snorting out the words. "It was contagious, you see. There was nothing we could do about it."

"I see."

"Tetsu. He came every single day. He brought that old watering can, even though it was so heavy, and he sprinkled medicine over the cats. The cats hated it, and they would scratch him. It was really hard work." As if to herself, she adds, "That

159

kid has grit," and nods. "But day by day, one would disappear and then another. Once he fell, watering can and all, spilling the medicine, and he burst into tears. 'That's enough,' I told him. 'Stop. There is nothing we can do to keep them from dying.' "

"And what did he do?"

She laughs a little. "He got mad. 'Even you say that!' he says. 'Well, I'm not giving up.' "

She takes her hand away from the sofa and the spring pops up again. "And you know, he didn't give up. It wasn't long after that that the sickness stopped. Like a typhoon that had blown past. It's funny, isn't it? It hit so suddenly, killed so many, then was gone as though nothing had happened. It was like something enormous had passed through."

I feel as though I can hear the sound of waves. The sound of waves, carrying something away, bringing something in. But it may just be the sound of the expressway.

"You know, sometimes there are things that you just can't do anything about," I say.

"Yup."

"But I'm glad Tetsu didn't give up, aren't you?"

She takes a deep breath. And then she roars out in her normal husky voice, "Of course!" and thumps me on the back. "To fight against something that you may not be able to do anything about, why, that's courage!"

I breathe in as deeply as I can. My heart, filled with the smells of summer, says farewell to this year's spring, already finished. I cannot describe very well what it is that Tetsu has done. But of the many things I encountered during the few days that I spent enough time with him to get heartily sick of him, not one was superfluous. The junk which other people discarded, the cats, the thunder, even the hate—if even one was missing, everything would have been different. This entire spring would have become something else. Now I no longer want to turn my eyes away from unpleasant things. Instead, I want to know everything: sad things, painful things, annoying things.

"Mom and Dad are getting along better now." The words slip from my mouth before I realize it. She looks a little surprised, but then says, "I see," and nods as she looks at the cats.

Someday I will tell her more about myself. And I will ask about her, too. I am sure it must be a long, long story. I want to know. I want to know more about this laughing lady with her flowered hat, who wears a white T-shirt beneath her worn sweatsuit. I want her to tell me about the boy in the photo. But little by little. Just as I am becoming an adult, little by little. I want to grow closer to her just as I gradually befriended the cats, slowly and carefully.

"We're moving tomorrow."

"Tetsu told me. He was all excited about going to school by bus. But it's just while you're rebuilding, right?"

"Yeah. We'll be back by the time it turns cold. Can we come visit you again?"

"Yes. I'll be waiting."

Tetsu appears from the shadow at the foot of one of the concrete pillars supporting the expressway. Both hands are bunched into fists, and he is practicing high karate kicks. A large gray cat, yawning lazily, walks nonchalantly in front of him as he approaches. Tail. He is better now, and quite fat. He has become one of the family. My father says he is going to sneak him into the apartment with us when we move. He and Tail often laze about together, as if they are kindred spirits.

"Tetsu has taken up karate. He goes three times a week."

Tetsu falls over backward on one of his high kicks, and Tail looks around, mewing short mews. Tetsu says something to the cat, stands up, and begins kicking again. The cat appears to be his karate instructor.

"He says he wants to be strong." The cat lady is watching him with her arms folded. "Well, it's going to be a hard road is my guess."

"You can say that again."

"But he says, 'When I get strong I won't let anyone lay a finger on you.' I wonder what he can be thinking of. I was so surprised . . . Why, Tomomi, what's wrong?"

I feel I am going to cry. I close my eyes tight and a ball of pure white light floats behind my eyelids. I close them tighter and tighter, then open them suddenly, and the sky is even bluer, and Tetsu, the cats, the woman, are all outlined, sharp and clear, in bright light.

"Now what? Why are you smiling like that?"

"Tetsu." I raise my voice, slightly embarrassed. "He knows the names of all the moves, even though he can't do most of them. All he reads these days is books about karate."

The lady stands up. "Tetsu! I'm off," she yells, and then begins pushing her bicycle up the slope of the embankment.

The grasses along the plain, grown very tall, have spread all over. An invisible river wind blows past, the grasses bending to mark its path. On and on forever. Above our sweat-beaded noses a swallow whizzes by.

The next day, after the moving truck leaves, carrying away Grandpa and my father, holding Tail in a basket, we drink iced barley tea, the only thing left in the house. My mother, Tetsu, and I are going by bus.

"This house will be demolished," Tetsu remarks. "I wish we could take it and keep it somewhere else instead."

My mother looks at Tetsu for a second and then laughs. "We will keep it," she says.

"Where?" Tetsu and I both ask at once.

"Here." She points to her chest. "I've lived here all my life, after all. I know every inch of this place. Even if I suddenly went blind, I would still know it."

"Let's try it, Mom." We wrap her apron round her eyes and tie it tight. Then she walks lightly around the house as if she can still see, announcing, "This is the light switch for the bathroom," or "This is where the stairs are." Even though everything has already been removed from the house, she moves her hands as if things are still there and she is stroking them, saying, "This is Grandpa's dresser," and "Here's the TV." Tetsu and I find this very funny and we walk beside her, our eyes half-closed, competing to be the first to shout, "Here's the kitchen table," "This is the closet. The iron is on the top shelf," "This is the nail where we hang the key to the front door," "This is where Tetsu drew on the wall," "Here's Grandma's chair" . . . Closing my eyes like this, I start to re-call other things, things that have long since disappeared from our house: Grandma's sewing machine, Tetsu's high chair when he was a baby. Sometimes the house creaks as if in answer to our voices.

It was a little after I got out of the hospital that the architectural drawings for our new house were finished. Perhaps my mother knew that I was debating whether or not I should ask her if she minded that the wall was staying in the same place. She looked steadily at me and then said flatly, "I am not going to think about that anymore. Our wall was always there, anyway. Is that all right with you, Tomomi?" I don't know what the adults decided among themselves, but I knew when I saw my mother's face that everything was going to be all right. And I had no complaints.

After we have done a complete circuit of the house we go out the back door, pulling our mother by the hand. While I struggle to open the door of the shed, the frame of which is slightly crooked, Tetsu wanders off toward the clothesline.

"I don't know the shed very well. Besides, everything has been taken out, hasn't it?" My mother starts to take off the blindfold but I ask her to leave it as it is.

The shed is completely cleaned out. The only thing left is the organ, disassembled and bound with cord.

"Kneel down, Mom." I place her hands on the board that used to be the organ lid.

"What could it be?" She tilts her head.

"It's yours."

She strokes it several times with her hands, checking its length, and then she smiles. "The organ. You mean we still

164

had it?" Removing the blindfold, she moves her fingers along the silent keyboard, as if playing a tune.

"What song is that?"

"I forget the name," she says, and then begins to sing softly. It is a quiet and very beautiful piece. "Your grandpa startled me by humming this one day, so I remember it well. It was the only time I ever heard him sing. He's always so shy about singing."

Singing "Desert Moon" together the night we slept in the bus is a secret just between Grandpa and me. "Maybe Grandpa is a lot like Dad."

"Maybe," my mother says, wrinkling her nose. "Maybe one of these days Dad'll get fat like Grandpa. Can you imagine that?"

I turn the corners of my mouth down and shake my head. My mother chuckles. I do, too. Kneeling there in the shed together, we laugh and laugh.

"Tomomi! Tomomi, come here a minute." Tetsu is calling me.

My mother stands up, saying, "Don't be long. We'll leave as soon as I've packed up the cups," and goes off toward the back door.

Tetsu stands with his back to me by the laundry poles, staring fixedly at something in the palm of his hand.

"What?"

I look over at the next-door neighbor's house. I haven't seen the old man in the yard since that day. Sometimes his wife comes out onto the veranda and combs her hair, peppered

165

with white and usually tightly tied in a bun, so slowly that it almost drives me crazy. The trees haven't been trimmed for a long time, and the cherry tree is covered in green leaves, while the oleander, blooming profusely, has stretched its heavy-looking branches above the roof of our shed.

"They were under the laurel tree." Tetsu turns toward me with his palms cupped together and gently opens his hands.

Eggs. Tiny eggs, less than one inch in length. There are three of them, all tinged with yellow.

"Birds' eggs?" I ask.

"I don't think so. They were in the grass shaded from the sun. They're probably—" Before he can finish, one of them begins to quiver. Tetsu and I freeze, staring. The egg cracks, a clear liquid dribbles out, and when finally a little slimy black lizard appears we both let out a whoop. We just can't help ourselves.

"Tetsu, let's take them to Reed Marsh. Our house is going to be torn down tomorrow."

"Good idea. They'll be all right there." He peers through his laced fingers into his hand. "I wonder what kind they are. I'll have to look them up in the encyclopedia."

"Don't break the other eggs."

"I know. I know."

Wonder, and something that can't be put into words, fills my body, becoming a shout. There is more than just a monster inside me. Like the baby lizard appearing from the egg, there are many other selves within me that I have not yet met, and it is enough to think that someday I may take each one of them by the hand.